I0604434

ALSO BY THE SAME AUTHOR

A MONTAGE OF A MAUVE REALITY
a collection of unusual short stories

TROUBLE IN MONATO
a fast-paced crime adventure with a sense of humour.

STAR-CROSSED
two people, two lives, one destiny.

FOR YOUR PLEASURE

&

QUESTIONABLE BEHAVIOUR

A Double Novella

Thomas James Taylor

for us all...

*we who endure the indifference and exploitation practised
by our governments & multi national business.*

CONTENTS

BOOK 1

QUESTIONABLE BEHAVIOUR

UNEXPECTED VISITORS

THE MORNING SUN slanted through a narrowly opened Venetian blind; bright shafts piercing the gloom, bending against angular objects resting on the living room floor: two portable television sets, three video recorders, a portable CD-player, a laptop computer, a small pile of gold and silver chains - some with pendants attached - a coin-jar three quarters full and a scatter of notes totalling around nine hundred dollars. A pizza box containing crusty remains.

Against one wall a television set delivered a picture unaccompanied by sound: an athletic-looking couple grinning inanely as they demonstrated the ease and fold away convenience of treadmills while a wooden company representative recited her spiel while the tee-vee personality intervened in with practised witticisms.

A low hiss filled the room, issuing from the speakers of a stereo system, alive but idle with tiny red and green lights gleaming in the shadows beneath the window. Over the steady hiss, the wheezing and snoring of two slumbering forms.

With his face pressed into the couch and one arm draped to the floor, lay Morris, his six and a half foot length leaving his feet protruding well past the armrest. Long, dark hair and beard framed a frowning countenance; a look suggesting perhaps some unresolved concern nettled even during sleep. The blue jeans, lace-up boots and black cotton shirt he wore accounted for the extent of his wardrobe, if not for the actual number of items in it.

Sideways in the room's one armchair slept Spider, a pale, wiry individual. His bald pate held the light, oily sheen of perspiration. Eyebrows almost comically arched steeply above the dark orbits of his eyes, while an aquiline nose gave a slightly predatory aspect to his features. His feet dangled over he arm of the chair, above the black thongs he had let fall to the floor before submitting to sleep. He was dressed in the jeans and navy blue, his common, year-round apparel. With his head thrown back and mouth opened wide, his eyes darted rapidly beneath dark lids as he dreamt of naked nymphs skiing fluidly down snow-covered slopes, himself in fervent pursuit.

It was hot outside. The neighbourhood lay still and quiet, stark beneath a brilliant blue sky and blazing sun. The street in front of number seven was entirely deserted. A hot breeze swirled dust and paper litter in the gutter as a shimmering heat haze rose from the bitumen, distorting Stobie-poles, footpaths, fences and houses along Clovelly Avenue, as if all was in the process of being melted down into a single, homogeneous, sticky puddle.

The sound of distant traffic ebbed and flowed in pulsing waves. A seaside suburb of Noarlunga, Christies Beach was a popular weekend destination in summer-time, or served at least as a passing-through point for weekend motorists headed for the southern coast, away from the more densely populated suburban Adelaide beaches. Cars of every size, shape, vintage and state of mechanical repair flowed along Beach Road, the town's main business centre, where tourist-reliant shopkeepers cluttered the sidewalks with inelegant signage; an attempt to catch the collective eye of prospective customers desperate to cash in on the tide of weekend pleasure- seekers with wage-packets opened and a myopic desire to find that elusive state of mind often spoken of but rarely discovered . . . happiness. A word spoken with reverence in these purlieus; a word almost mythological in nature and spoken most-always in the past tense as reminiscent recollections of a distant past.

At the coast Beach Road met The Esplanade at a T-junction. Those intending to visit generally veered right to begin the often arduous task of finding a vacant parking space; a frustrating endeavour, occasionally leading to heated disputes with other drivers likewise engaged; each insisting they had claimed the space first. Fist-fights on such occasions were not unheard of.

On particularly busy days local residents could find themselves prevented from leaving their homes, stymied by vehicles whose thoughtless or plain ignorant occupants, transcending all reason, deemed it necessary to park across their driveways. The offending vehicles were to be seen smartly being towed away by city council employees, happy to work the overtime rates and generate the extra revenue for them selves and the Corporation of the City of Onkaparinga.

To turn left at The Esplanade led over the steep-sided prominence known as Whitton Bluff. The strip of bitumen arched over the hulking mass to Port Noarlunga and on, stretching to the abundant, white sand beaches along the south coast of the Fleurieu Peninsula. Along this route the more youthful motorists were want to cruise, stereo systems blaring with the latest of musical compositions of the generation, tossing out fast food packaging and soft drink containers along the way in cool and carefree abandon.

Against the southbound flow of traffic travelled a white LTD Ford. Behind the wheel sat a man by the name of Edward Madden, aka Mad Eddy, aka Nails. His face was well tanned behind mirror sun-glasses, his dark hair cropped short. In the air-conditioned interior of his immaculately maintained car he wore a lightweight sports jacket over a white T-shirt, blue jeans and white sneakers. Entering the outskirts of Port Noarlunga from the south side he leaned across to turn down the stereo which played his favourite Kevin Borich collection, retrieved the cigarette he had placed behind his ear before departing home and lit up. At Ward Street, adjacent to the Port Noarlunga Hotel, he swung left and halfway along the short street pulled up out front a white, stucco-finished house with a verandah running along its full length. Half a minute later a very large man of Polynesian extraction emerged from the house into the daylight.

Spider's snow nymphs proved fo be swift and infuriatingly elusive. No matter how desperately he willed himself forward at ever greater speed, he was no match for the nubile beauties who seemed to mock his efforts as they descended the slope in easy, fluent arcs, their taut, round buttocks wiggling tormentingly in font him.

A thump on the arm woke him instantly. His eyes sprang open to find Morris looming over him, a sardonic grin drawn to one side of his face.

"What you moanin' about?"

"Eh, what?" Spider muttered, annoyed and trying to gather his wits.

"All that groaning. You dreaming about chicks again, you incorrigible bastard?"

"No," he protested innocently. "It was, er... I don't remember now."

"Never known anybody so tail crazy," Morris continued, ignoring the denial. "Except maybe for Tassie Pete, and I don't even like to think what happened to *him*."

"What?" Spider righted himself in the armchair. "What happened to Tassie Pete?"

Morris shook his head ruefully and walked off in the direction of the kitchen. "You don't want to know, buddy. You don't want to know."

Unexpectedly, he found what he had gone for laying atop the kitchen table and not at all where it should have been. A small, metal film canister lying open and empty, spoons, syringes and other paraphernalia scattered around.

"Spider!" he called, staring angrily at the evidence.

Spider entered the kitchen behind him, his singlet off and slung over one shoulder. "Fuck it's hot," he expressed emphatically. "Fuck that," Morris responded, turning to face him. "What the bloody hell is this?" He hooked a thumb over his shoulder, in the direction of the table. "Tell me you didn't finish off the dope last night."

Spider spread his arms wide; an innocent repose, nonplussed. "Me? . . . Man, don't you remember? We finished it about half three this morning. Both of us! There wasn't much left and we figured we'd just do it and score again today."

Morris reflected for a moment. There *was* a vague memory. "Fuck it," he said at last, and went to the refrigerator for a beer.

"I feel like shit." He popped open the tab and Spider watched as he gulped the lot down in one go.

"Does that really help?"

"Doesn't hurt."

Morris reached for another. "Want one?" Spider shrugged. "Why not?"

He didn't usually drink this early, but already he felt the slight unpleasantness that told him he would need another fix quite soon. "Is it hot, or is it just me?"

"It's hot," Morris confirmed, handing him the last beer. "And we got to get our butts into gear today."

The two of them returned to the lounge room where Spider flicked on the light switch to better inspect the night's haul. Morris turned off the television set and reaching into the bottom recess of the cabinet it sat on, pulled out a hookah, the bowl of which contained a small amount of cannabis.

Spider stood with arms folded. "We did alright. Better unload this lot before the list goes out. "Glenelg?" he suggested.

By Glenelg he meant the suburb, and the pawnbroker there who ran the shop on Jetty Road.

There were half a dozen pawnbrokers and second-hand merchants they used in and around the city. All were reasonably accommodating; that is, if they provided suitable I.D. There were no questions asked, but they were mindful not to transgress the tacit understanding not to frequent one business too regularly, thereby minimising the odds of police proving culpability on the part of the proprietor should things go awry.

"Glenelg it is," Morris agreed. "Let's hope he takes the lot. In that case we'll go on to West Beach and see if we can't score off Max."

Spider gave a quizzical look. "I thought Max was busted."

"Max gets busted on a regular basis. Not officially, though, if you know what I mean."

The blank look on Spider's face indicated that he had no idea. Morris took a breath.

"Max got busted, big time, a couple of years back. Like he was supplying half the users in the city via the dealers who scored off of him, you know? The young, ambitious and aspiring drug squad members of the day, the ones looking to climb up through the ranks, they realised that if they took him out of the picture, in one fell swoop they'd be halving the necessity for their own positions. Back then, the Government was cutting back on everything. Still are, the mongrels. But by stopping Max, they recognised they might be cutting their own throats, see? So, what the coppers did, they offered him a deal; rolled him over. A lesser charge, a word in the prosecutor's ear and the beak lets him walk."

"He got off?" Spider's eyebrows jumped high in surprise.

"No, not off," Morris explained gravely. "*On*, as in *on* the hook. And there ain't no gettin' off unless the coppers let him off. Not likely.

"Max sells as much dope as he wants, unmolested ... sanctioned, if you like. The coppers make more busts through him than they could ever hope to on their own. Good arrest rates equals continued employment and even promotions. Just enough junkies at large to keep the show on the road. As for his occasional arrests, well, it's not hard to work out, is it?"

Spider had listened to the explanation very carefully, his expression, however, indicated there was some uncertainty. "What?" he asked.

"It's a farce. Bogus. A sham!

"Listen, mate... anyone arrested for dealing smack as many times as he was should not still be in business, let alone walking the streets. I'm telling you, those so-called busts are a put-up job, designed to maintain his credibility in the game."

Spider whistled through his teeth. "Max is a rat?"

"A survivor might be a better description," Morris hedged.

He brought the pipe to his lips, set light to the green wad stuffed in the cone, drew deep and hard.

"Why would you do business with a rat?" Spider wanted to know. But Morris was busy filling his lungs with smoke and couldn't answer.

While Spider waited for a response, from the front door there came an odd scratching sound, much like a dog scratching to come indoors. Only they didn't have a dog. He went to investigate.

The instant he turned back the latch, Spider found himself being thrust backwards behind the swinging door, a huge Polynesian man doing the thrusting. Unsure whether to run or fight, he waited ambivalently.

Morris had risen quickly from the couch; to do what, he wasn't sure. A great cloud of smoke burst from his lungs in a sudden fit of coughing, air now his primary concern.

Behind the Polynesian came Edward Madden, cool and calmly collected as he stepped into the room. A Cheshire cat grin broadening across his face, exposing very white teeth as he slipped off his sun-glasses.

"Hello, lads," he addressed them pleasantly, and his eyes fell immediately to the collection of cash and goods occupying the centre of the living room floor.

"Hey, I'm impressed. You know, I was just telling Lokki here what an enterprising pair the two of you are, and how unusual it is for you not to pay me what you owe on time. Morris?" There was menace in his tone.

Morris was still coughing hard, unable to adequately respond. His eyes streamed tears and seemed about to pop from their sockets. He was forced to sit back down on the couch and wrap his arms around his chest in effort to regain composure.

Madden ignored his plight, instead crouching beside the booty and picking out a gold chain and locket which had caught his eye. Lokki, meanwhile, suggested to Spider that he might like to sit beside his friend: this by way of a nod, to which Spider agreed without much deliberation.

"I like this," Madden intoned expressively, affecting delight as he let the small locket swing at the end of the chain.

"Oh, yes. You know, I think this would go just fine with Gloria's new dress. That okay, Morris?"

He glanced to Morris who by now was beginning to breathe easier. "Thanks, mate."

Slipping the piece into his pocket as he stood, he went to the vacant armchair and seated himself in a leisurely manner. He brought his fingers together to form an arch just below eye-level while regarding Morris and Spider who now sat side by side on the couch.

"I was about to give you a call, Eddie," Morris managed. "I've got almost all the cash I owe you. We were about to convert this lot into readies. Should have it done by three o'clock-*ish*, I'd say." Madden nodded unconcernedly. "You've done quite well. Let me guess where it came from. Willunga, perhaps?"

"Aldinga," Spider volunteered, keen to preserve the mood of congeniality.

Madden chuckled. "Poor old Aldinga, eh? Whenever will the pollies provide adequate policing down that way? It really is a shame. Retirees mostly, aren't they. Work all your life dutifully paying taxes and what consideration do you get at the end of it all? I'm surprised there's any meat left on that old carcass, though. Thought it was all picked over."

Morris's attention was with Lokki who had moved to casually inspect the record collection on top of a speaker box: a practiced manoeuver. But here was a topic of interest.

"And so does everyone else think the same. Only the easy pickings though. The ones with anything to protect have invested in security: barred windows, security fences and such. Ineffectual. Stupid really. Makes it so much easier to pick out your target. The most basic of tools and ten minutes extra work is all it takes. The reward is always greater."

"Audacious," Madden replied, and decided he liked the word. "Audacious. You're an *audacious* man, Morris. That's why I've always liked you. You're your own man."

"So. . ." said Morris, sensing something unsettling, and he reached for the can of beer by his feet. "Three o'clock okay?" and he took a good draught.

"The deadline was yesterday. Noon, yesterday," Madden pointed out, as if addressing an inattentive child. "You missed the deadline."

Before Morris could reply, Spider intervened. "Hey, Eddie. Do you got any dope? I ain't feelin' so good."

"You do look a bit pasty, Spider." He paused, thoughtful for a moment. "We'll talk about that in a bit, shall we? First things first. Business takes priority."

Spider was visibly disappointed and seemed about to pursue the subject further, but the disapproving scowl from his companion moved him to remain silent.

"We'd have had the dough days ago," Morris resumed, "but we couldn't rush this one. Tricky. There were a number of factors to be considered."

"I appreciate that fact, Morris. I do. It's not the easiest occupation to be in. It takes *nouse*, I know."

"So what's going on here? I don't see the problem."

Madden lowered his hands and meshed his fingers over his chest.

"Business is what's going on here. And business is business."

Frustration showed in Morris's darkening face. He reached again for his beer can, realised it was empty and tossed it against the far wall reflexively.

"Out of fucking beer," he growled. "All right, Eddie. What is it you want?"

Madden reached into his pocket and pulled out a fifty-dollar note. "Lokki," he said, proffering the money toward the big man. "Would you mind? Nip over to the pub and get us some beers." Lokki moved languidly to accept the money. In crossing to the door he left Morris and Spider with a parting look needing no translation.

"Good man, Lokki," Madden commented when the door had closed.

"Doesn't say much," Morris observed.

"Doesn't need to," Madden countered conversationally. Champion rugby player, you know. Or was 'til he broke a man's back and got himself barred for life."

"Let me guess." said Morris. "You found him working as a doorman at some wanky night-club."

Madden's response was instant laughter; genuine, but suppressed to the point where it emerged as something of a giggle. "Absolutely correct," he tittered. "Fucking audacious, Morris. Absolutely on the money. Hey, check this out."

In a flash he had drawn a gun and was pointing it midway between the two. It gleamed menacingly in the sparse light of the room; so too his eyes.

"Ain't it a beaut? Rhuger thirty-eight, rapid-fire. Cost me a five spot, but worth it don't you think?"

"Yeah, terrific," Morris replied anxiously. Spider seemed perplexed. "A real investment."

He slipped it back into the holster under his arm, where it was neatly concealed by his jacket.

"Now, let's talk," he said, leaning forward as if about to impart an intimate secret.

"There are two things in your favour, Morris. One, this is the first time you have let me down. Though once is enough," he added pointedly. "I don't often give people second chances, *you* know that. And secondly, as I said before, I do like you Morris. I'm being sincere when I say that. I like your independent attitude, your ability to achieve what you put your mind to. In spite of your chosen profession and one or two small vices, I know that deep down you're an honourable and capable man. Honour is quite a rare thing these days, don't you think? Commendable, and something I feel needs to be taken into account here."

He paused, searched his pockets and pulled out a packet of cigarettes and a lighter. "You boys want a smoke?"

Madden got out of his chair to stand over them as he offered them their cigarettes. Provided a light, then returning to his chair and lighting his own cigarette, he resumed in a friendly manner.

"Say if I were to overlook this one blemish, lads. Would you do something for me in return? I mean as an act of mutual goodwill, like. Tit for tat."

"Such as?" Morris asked, wishing he could avoid the whole conversation. This whole damned pantomime was pissing him of immensely.

"Just a small thing, really. A former business associate you could say. Only, he left my employ with something not belonging to him." The manifestation of some bitter emotion flickered across his face and was gone. "I'd like the two of you to pay a visit, visit with him awhile. You know the sort of thing," he sneered. He took a draw of his cigarette, reached forward to crush it out in the ashtray.

"You want him knocked about," Morris clarified.

"I want what belongs to me," Madden replied without expression. "*How*, is your responsibility. You do this for me and your debt is paid up, cleared. Plus, two grams of smack and five hundred apiece on delivery. What do you say to that?"

"What if the guy won't come across?"

"He will," Madden said adamantly, holding Morris unwaveringly in his gaze. "It's a generous offer. Very generous, considering the alternative," he stressed mildly, while adjusting his coat beneath which the Rhuger bulged slightly.

"I'll tell you what. You guys talk it over while I go take a slash." He rose, headed towards the kitchen. "End of the hallway, is it?"

"Down the end and left," Spider obliged, and when he was sure that Madden was out of earshot, he prodded Morris with his elbow. "Our lucky day or what? What a friggin' break."

"Yeah, lucky," Morris responded, gloomily.

"What's the matter? It'll be a piece of cake. Just put the *frighteners* on some schmuck, snaffle the whatever-it-is and we're back in business . And three grand up!"

"Two and a half, actually," Morris corrected. "But I don't know-" "Don't know? What's not to know? I'm definitely in. And don't forget the two grams. Man, I need a taste, *bad*."

"You ever do anything like this before, Spider?"

"Yeah. Lots of times," he expressed indignantly, but Morris regarded him amusedly, doubt evident in his grey eyes.

"Well, once. One time, maybe two." Spider amended.

"Once before? You sure about that?"

Spider nodded soberly. "Once before, Morris. One time."

Morris shook his head slowly. "This is one lousy way to start a day. No dope, no beer, a shit-load of stolen goods to cart across the city on a stinking hot day, and Nails bloody Madden down on us to do him some grubby little favour. I ain't in the bloody mood for this shit. Not in the mood at all."

"You reckon we got a choice?" Spider replied, less a question than an observation.

Lokki pushed open the front door, a carton of beer clutched under one very large arm. By fluke or design, the beer was Morris's favourite brand.

Madden re-entered from the passageway as Lokki placed the carton on the floor at the centre of the room.

"*Ahh* ... refreshments," he enthused. He strode over to the carton and tore open the top, pulled a can free and reseated himself in the armchair.

Morris looked at the carton in deliberation. Plainly, to accept was to move a step closer toward Eddie Madden's odious sphere of control. But then, wasn't it already a bit late for that? No more after this, he determined. He would clear his debt with Madden and never again allow himself to be put in such a compromising position. Not with Eddie, and not with any other tin-plated gangster.

"Screw it," he said, rising and helping himself to two cans of beer.

"What's the story with this caper?"

Madden produced a thin smile, took a small sip from his can. Then, banging it loudly down on the wooden end of the armrest, leaned forward, the better to impart the story.

"This person's name," he began, and the word *person* he expressed with particular emphasis, "is Miles Joseph Owen. He was my accountant, up until six days ago. He has in his possession a number of bearer bonds and a few other paper assets worth a considerable amount. They're mine and I want them back. That's your job. Couldn't be easier."

It *was* straightforward enough, but Morris looked somewhat puzzled. "Why do you need us? From where I sit, I gather you like to take care of business yourself."

"You're quite right, Morris. I do believe in the personal touch. Only; well, this time I want to take a more subtle approach, to make a point. I want this *person* to know that he's not worthy of my direct attention, see? Implied indifference if you like."

"You mean so he thinks you ain't too bothered about it," Spider chipped in, looking pleased with himself.

Madden's eyes narrowed. "That's very good, Spider. But do shut up, there's a good fellow."

Spider's moment of pleasure turned instantly to sullenness. His eyes darted from person to person, searching either for sympathy or that tell-tale look which signaled derision. People were always mocking him to his face without a thought. Even when he wasn't in the room he knew they made fun of him and said he was a dummy.

"It's cool," Morris said consolingly. "Eddie's just a bit stressed, that's all. But, yeah, so he doesn't think he's too bothered. That's right. That's exactly it, buddy."

Madden tried to ignore the interruption, but when Morris turned his attention back to him there seemed to be something vaguely unsettling in his demeanour. He dismissed it, produced a notepad and pen from his pocket, wrote hurriedly and tore off the page, setting it on the table before Morris.

"There's the address. Fourteen, The Esplanade. It's right near the top of the bluff. Tonight would be good. Say around nine."

"Will he be alone?" Morris asked.

"He lives alone," he replied. "Saturday nights he stays in. He has a hobby with records or something, he told me. Drinks wine and plays records. Count Basie, Miles Davis and all that. You guys can handle this, right?"

Morris picked up the piece of paper on which the address was scrawled, looked hard at it for a moment before shoving it into his pocket. "Lean on the guy 'til he hands over the bearer bonds. Yeah, okay. I suppose we could manage it," he said, sounding excessively put upon.

Madden pushed himself to his feet. "I know you lads won't let me down. Go in at nine o'clock. I'll be nearby and I'll ring you from my mobile after I've given you some time. Oh, and a word of advice. This guy is a shocking liar. Couldn't lie straight in bed, as they say. Typical accountant, eh?" he chuckled. "You're there for one thing only, remember.

My property ... no freelancing. He'll bleat and squeal and he'll say any damn thing, but you don't leave there without it, right?"

Morris gave a curt nod. "Yeah, okay." "Good," said Madden, making for the door.

Spider made half a gesture to him but hesitated, instead turning plaintively to Morris.

"You said you'd do us some dope, Eddie," Morris reminded him. "Oh, yeah. I nearly forgot," Madden replied, stopping short of the door and searching the inside breast pocket of his sports jacket. "Two hundred do?"

"Yeah. Two hundred will do fine."

He pulled open the front door. "Lokki, duck out to the car and get a gram, would you?"

With Lokki's departure there was silence. Morris rose, went to the collection of money on the floor and began counting out the two hundred from the ten and twenty dollar notes.

Watching on, Madden commented, "I've noticed your habit is costing you more these days. Perhaps you should consider kicking for a while."

"That's some advice, coming from you," said Morris, squaring off the notes into a neat bundle.

"Hey, I don't make people use the stuff. They use, okay? I just supply what they want, and there are risks involved in doing that, you know. Besides, if it wasn't me, it'd be someone else, right?" Morris was weighing up the pros and cons of replying to this when Lokki returned from the car. From his pocket he withdrew the one gram packet of heroin, neatly contained in a small plastic pouch, and handed it to Morris.

Morris passed the money to Madden without comment. "Nine o'clock,

"Madden said, stepping across the threshold. "Nine," Morris agreed.

By 11a.m. they were rolling contentedly along Lonsdale Highway, the Combie loaded with the plundered goods and maintaining a steady, puttering 90 k.p.h., all other northbound traffic flowing swiftly past them.

The heat inside the metal shell of the van was stifling, though it seemed not to affect Spider at all. Morris, on the other hand, sweated profusely, his black cotton shirt soaked and his already sore and bloodshot eyes stinging as perspiration trickled from his brow.

Cranking down the window and opening the vent brought only limited relief. Hot air blasted in off the scorching highway: eminently efficient in drying uncomfortable, sodden clothing; bloody annoying in the way it caused his hair to lash about his face. In winding the glass back up again, it jammed halfway; and applying extra force to budge it, the handle broke off from the spindle.

"Beer," Morris said, the effort of self-control affecting his voice as he slung the offending object through the half open window.

Spider rode with his feet pushed up on the dash. He reached down between his legs and lifted the lid of the cooler, crammed full with ice and cans of beer. Popping one open, he handed it to his friend who accepted it without taking his eyes off the road.

"Ta," he said, and took a relieving sip, just as a metallic green HQ Holden loaded with youths drew alongside. The two on the near side were leaning out of windows, shouting abusively. Apparently the jettisoned handle had upset them somehow. Morris shrugged and made an apologetic gesture with one hand, but, unappeased, the youths continued their vitriolic fusillade.

"I don't need this," he expressed wearily, but Spider was already on the move.

He climbed into the back of the van and hurriedly rooted around among the collection of miscellaneous tools and accumulated odds and ends, finally coming up with a tin of black gloss enamel paint, which he quickly prized the lid off of.

Morris, having adjusted his rear-view mirror to see what he was up to, chuckled as he guessed his intent. "I'll try and get a bit ahead of 'em," he said over his shoulder. "I'll tell you when." In order to keep the lads interested, he contorted his face and applied the universally understood one-fingered salute. The effect was to bring the car threateningly closer, at which point Morris accelerated.

"Now would be good," he called, and Spider slid back the side door and let fly with the tin of paint.

The result surpassed expectation. The tin struck squarely in the centre of the bonnet, splattering black paint over the expensive paintwork and splashing across the whole windscreen, leaving the driver no option but to pull over immediately. The look of shock and surprise on the faces of those in the car had Morris and Spider howling with laughter, and the remainder of the journey was travelled in high spirits.

At Glenelg, Morris turned off of Jetty Road and reversed the van in behind an old red brick building.

COSMO'S QUALITY SECOND-HAND AND PAWNBROKER, read the sign.

The traditional three metal balls hung prominently above from an ornate wrought iron bracket.

"You want to stay with the gear while I go in?" Morris asked. "Thieves, you know. Can't trust no one these days."

Spider agreed, and watched as his friend ambled off towards the rear door of the premises. After a moment he leaned forward and switched on the radio, twisted the tuning knob in search of anything of interest.

Inside, Morris wended his way through the cluttered stock. Everything from antique secretaries and crystal chandeliers to bedpans and broomsticks were piled high on either side of narrow access ways. The nearer he drew to the front of the shop, the cleaner and tidier everything became, until he arrived at the central display area, stocked with good quality furniture and electrical goods, a long rank of refrigerators edging one perimeter with a similar line of washing machines adjoining.

Near the front entrance a young woman attended to a female customer interested in an item of jewellery housed in the glass display cabinet. A young man with a bottle of correction fluid busied himself in the white goods section, deftly covering over chips and scratches in the enamelled surfaces.

The man he had come to see appeared on his left from a parallel aisle, garbed in brown slacks, plaid jacket and sporting a trilby hat.

Short in stature and being what some people might describe as a bit on the podgy side, still, his features presented a somewhat curious appearance. Leonard Cosmo McLeary always put Morris in mind of an aging cherub - though in all of the twenty years he had known him, he seemed to have aged not in the slightest. His skin looked smooth and unusually soft, and his face, although Morris knew him to be fifty three years old, was imbued with some indefinable youthful quality.

He led a young couple across the floor in the direction of a white leather lounge suite, extolling its "virtually new" condition and telling how its previous owner, a rich, well-to-do widow of some celebrity had often entertained V.I.P.'s while reposed on this very suite, and several famous names passed glibly from his lips. At the mention of "His Royal Highness, Prince Charles", and "the Right Honourable Sir Desmond Tutu,"the spiel was interrupted by hoarse laughter.

Morris did his level best to control himself as McLeary and his prospective buyers turned to observe him animatedly slapping his chest in an affected bout of coughing.

"Must be the dust," he tried, wheezing unconvincingly. McLeary's baby-blues narrowed. "Why don't I let the two of you talk it over for a while, while I see if I can assist this gentleman?"

McLeary strode over to where Morris's charade fast-deteriorated into laughter again. In an outward show of concern he took Morris by the arm and, with a surprisingly firm grip which lent a sobering effect, led Morris in the direction of his office.

"You big galoot," McLeary hissed beside him. "That suite is worth a packet, and I haven't made a single sale this morning."

"Sorry, Lenny," Morris chuckled. "But Desmond Tutu was a bit much, wasn't it?"

Lenny gave him a sideways glance as he opened the door and nudged Morris through. "We'll see, shall we?" A trace of a smile smoothed his countenance. "Twenty bucks says they bite." He pointed Morris to a worn but comfortable-looking chair as he rounded the desk and took up position in his own, plushly upholstered, swivel model.

Morris gave a sigh. "Lenny, I"m trying to accumulate, not-"

"Oh dear, *moosh*. Doing it a bit tough, are we?" Light danced in McLeary's eyes. "Alright, ten?"

"Yeah, okay," Morris relented. "If I must."

"Right then. Now-" McLeary pushed himself up straight in his chair. "Let's to business. What you got that I might want?"

...

TIME OUT

L ATER THAT DAY, around three-thirty, in fact, the lads made their way to Brighton Beach. McLeary had taken what they had to offer and paid $490 in the bargain; ten dollars being subtracted from the initial $500 when, at the last minute, the young couple decided on the white leather lounge suite. So miffed had Morris been, he *lifted* a pair of deck-chairs and a beach umbrella from the rear of the shop in departure, and with nothing else on the agenda until the coming evening, a relaxing interlude at the seaside presented itself as a not altogether unsatisfactory way of whiling away these few hours.

The umbrella Morris stole was printed with the twelve signs of the zodiac, gold on blue, and beneath this the two reclined in the matching chairs, Morris with a can of beer held to his chest as he peered thoughtfully out to the horizon, and Spider surveying the beach with a pair of purloined binoculars, eagerly zeroing in on the numerous, scantily clad women adorning the foreshore. While Spider occupied his mind with thoughts of rather a lascivious nature, Morris's train of thought took a more meandrine and introspective course as, in rare leisurely moments such as this, they were sometimes wont to do:

I'm forty years old - too bloody old to be existing this way. A bloke ought to have a nice, quiet little place in the coun-

try, a crop of marijuana, home- brewed beer, a dog and some other animals. Maybe even a woman. I gotta kick this habit! Maybe I could get a job in a country garage somewhere, fixing cars and trucks, farm machinery even... "Hey, Morris! Hank Jones has got a problem with the transmission on his Massey Ferguson. Want to take a drive out and check it over?"

"Still owes us on the ute from a mouth ago, don't he?"

"It can wait. Crop's ready for harvest and there's rain on the way."

"Right, I'm on it."

Old farmer Jones would be pleased as hell to see me comin' down the track. Help is here, Jonesy. You' ll have your harvest in and time to spare. Not a problem for an old spanner-head like me.

A dorsal fin split the water's surface about sixty metres offshore. Another others! Five dolphin in all.

It's a nice day. Hot. Hot as Hades. Yeah, a nice day in hell. I like the heat. Much rather cook than freeze. Those cold nights in Perth back in '74, no digs, no nothin'. Walking the streets all night just to keep warm. Walking the streets all day, knocking door to door for odd jobs, trying to raise enough dough for a meal and a bed. Damn near starved. Would've, had I not walked into the headquarters of one of the biggest mining outfits in the country. The North-West, now that's hot!

He drained his can and reached into the ice-box for another. Spider, he noticed without much concern, was still wholly occupied with the optic nerve. He sipped from the fresh can and sighed quietly, settled back and allowed himself to slip once more into reverie: *There might be a few years' work in the old dog yet. Time enough to put some money away - a nest-egg. But maybe I'm too far gone already. I feel* pretty stuffed not sure I've got it in me any more. I gotta clean up my act.

I'd have liked to be an astronomer no, a cosmologist. Delve the mysteries of the universe, find out what makes it all tick. The big bang, the big crunch and all that. Or is it all delicately poised, set to reach perfect balance and continue endlessly? Will it all fade into entropy, thermal exhaustion, and die to be forever lost? And we puny creatures, what importance will our fleeting moment have been at the end? Is all in vain and without purpose, a desperate struggle to cling to existence in denial of nature's law which demands a beginning and an end to all things? But the in between - from the spark of creation to the snuffing out of the final flame - what a game what challenges exist! A cosmologist, yes, and maybe a theologian, too. To plumb the depths of possibility, explore the convoluted pathways of logic and weave webs glistening with sophistry; a tapestry which, to pull the single, master thread would bring it all undone, revealing the great illusion.

And what of God? Did mankind create God out of fear of the unknown? Is there room for such a concept in light of what is understood of the creative forces at work within the cosmos? The whole thing could go back to primal man and his childlike capacity for wonder. His intuitive sense of the existence of a creative force in action. Countless generations of man striving to understand and explain it, put a name to it; that mysterious something which seemed ever destined to elude comprehension, or, at least, uniform belief in any one proposition.

Such inquisitive little creatures, people: who? what? where? when? why? how? ... got to have the answers. Can't simply exist, be happy with what's at hand. Never happy with *only what is at hand. Must have more or better ... some, just because another has some. What a pathetic lot.*

"Hey, Morris. Check out the tits on this."

"Not now, Spider, I'm thinking."

A momentary feeling of sickness washed over Morris. He had a strong urge to throw up but he resisted until it passed. The combination of beer and heroin often had this effect.

Bloody Spider and his obsession with sex. Silly bugger. Twenty three and probably never had a fuck. Ain't missin' much. But if I told him that he'd only think I was bullshitting and being patronising. Guess I shouldn't let on that I know all his stories are bullshit, it'd only undermine his self-esteem. Got little enough as it is!

Mental note: get Spider laid before he does something really stupid. I'll take him to a whore-house next time we get a decent haul... least I can do for the guy. Should never have brought him in with me. Enough thieves around already ... but, shit, there ain't a chance he could look after himself. Grist for the mill, as they say. Man, I've got to cut him loose, teach him to stand on his own. "Spider, I never asked you nothin' personal before, but you must have some family somewhere, do you?

"Nuh. Dead," he replied, lowering the binoculars and meeting Morris's squinting countenance.

"Brothers, sisters?"

"Had a twin brother. Watched him go under a train when we were nine."

"That's rough. I'm sorry. Jesus, Spider, that's pretty heavy. Must trouble you some."

"Sometimes," Spider said thoughtfully. "Means I gotta live for both of us now. And..." But then he hesitated, a look on his face which indicated he had crossed into difficult territory.

"Go on, buddy. And ... ?"

Morris waited, deciding not to prompt him further as Spider sheepishly avoided his gaze. Then, having reached some inner decision, he took a breath and looked up.

"Half of me is missing," he said sadly. "The half that's him. When I die, too, we'll be whole again. But don't try and figure it, no one else never can see there's no other way. They say I gotta be just me, develop my *I n d I v I d u a l I t y.*

"You've seen a shrink then?"

"Yeah. That's what they say but they don't know but from books." "No," Morris agreed. "How could they? Man, that's a real shitty deal."

Spider shrugged, turned towards the ocean. "His name was Taran."

The connection hit Morris like a punch in the head. *Taran.* In the school yard Taran would easily become *Tarantula,* and from there, no doubt, become *"Spider".*

"I never had any siblings," was all Morris could utter in reply, and the subject was dropped by tacit agreement.

I hope old Spidie ain't a tad schizo. Still, he's harmless enough. Jake the bloody snake, he was a schizo. Hell of a laugh to drink with but a bit of a worry and a thieving bastard to boot. Couldn't trust him. Paranoid schizophrenic. Delusions. Thought he was a bloody werewolf. No fun living with a werewolf, for a cert. Watching someone eat a kilo of raw meat can be a little disconcerting Not hard to detect a lycanthrope: smelliest farts, ever!

On the subject of evil smells: Eddie bloody Madden. Looks like the son of a bitch has finally maneuvered me into *working for him. How much do I owe him? $1,200, right. I had nine hundred, less two hundred for the dope. That's seven. Five hundred from Lenny, less the ten for the flamin' lounge suite. That's eleven hundred and ninety bucks. Damn - can't even buy my way out! Suppose I've already committed myself anyway. Your mother gave birth to a prize idiot, it seems. An idiot who stands by his word, unfortunately.*

"Hey, Morris."

"Hmmm?"

"What happened to Tassie Pete?"

"Tassie Pete?" Morris fought to shake off the drug-induced sleepiness.

"Yeah, remember? You were sayin' this morning how this guy was tail- crazy and that something happened to him."

"Oh, yeah." Morris's face developed a sly smile. He took a sip from his can and opened his eyes. "Tassie Pete."

The question of Tassie Pete had been tormenting Spider since that morning. Vexingly, Morris had failed to adequately respond. He had waited until now to raise the question again, in hope that now might be the right time, and by the way Morris straightened himself in his chair and reached for a cigarette, the signs were indeed promising.

Morris lit the cigarette, well aware of Spider's long-endured test of patience, and savouring the moment, teasingly stretched it a while longer, drawing deeply, exhaling the smoke in an exaggerated and leisurely manner. He had Spider's full attention.

"In '83 I once stopped over in Coober Pedy. I was hitchin' down from Darwin and I got stuck there late one rather chilly afternoon. Couldn't get a decent long ride so I went to the nearest pub to fill in time 'til morning. I ended up stayin' there for three months, lendin' a hand to work this fellah's opal mine while his partner recovered after falling down a shaft. He had staggered away from the campfire one night, to take a piss. Of course he had been drinking since knock-off. Just wasn't paying attention.

"Casper, that was the guy I worked for. He had a wife back down south. She refused to come up and rough it but didn't mind waitin' while hubby dug up a fortune in coloured rock; and most of the money he made he was sending down to her, to squirrel away. He told me about the dude I was fillin' in for. His name was Pete. Came from Tasmania.

"We were at the pub, drinking off the effects of a week's hard yakka down a bloody hole. Tassie Pete, it turned out, was pretty well known around the parts. Everyone had a story to tell about his reputation, his exploits with the women. Old Casper thought it was a bit of alright. Being a fairly quiet old dude, he enjoyed having a sidekick of some note, dubious though it may be. Everyone enjoys *some* form of notoriety in *Coober*. Most all of the other blokes thought it was a bit of a chuckle, too. All but them whose wives this Pete character had been visiting, understandably. The story was he had a monster of a dick. You know, a thing like that spikes the girls' interest.

"Anyway, Pete had to be flown down to Adelaide for hospitalisation, and seeing as how he was there, and seeing as he was Casper's partner, Laura, that's Casper's wife, would occasionally drop in to visit at his bedside. And as one might expect, she offers to put him up at home during the final stages of his recovery. With Casper's approval, naturally. Casper was a top bloke."

Spider's eyes widened. "You gonna tell me they-"

"Exactly," Morris nodded, blowing smoke in a leisurely manner. "This gutter-crawler had an affair with his partner's wife, while *he* was up there slavin' his guts out, making money for them all." "And Casper found out?"

"Casper had many friends back in Adelaide, but he was smart enough not to act merely on hearsay. He was already suspicious, I guess. His partner's injuries were taking a little too long to mend so he hired a P.I. and, well, sure enough, the stories proved quite true. You can imagine how he felt about that."

"What'd he do?" Spider asked eagerly.

"What would you have done, had you been cuckold?" Morris countered evasively. He much enjoyed keeping Spider suspended.

"Eh?"

"Back-doored," he amended. "Cuckold is when someone's missus is being secretly shafted by another bloke."

Spider thought on it for a second or two before declaring angrily, "I'd cut his balls off!"

"Really?" Morris regarded his friend musingly. Is that right?"

"Too right," Spider insisted.

Just the reply he had anticipated. Morris allowed himself a smug grin, another draw on the cigarette before resuming.

"I reckon Casper must have brooded on it for a couple of weeks, because in that time he got to not sayin' much. Less than usual, I mean. Just worked like a demon and said bugger all that wasn't related to running a safe, smooth operation. Had a well-ordered mind and was as dogged as they come. Got to be in that game. So even then I wasn't really aware that anything was up.

"Then one day he says its time to knock off for no apparent reason. It was two in the afternoon and we'd only been back at it an hour or so, and he says, let's knock off and we'd have a few beers. What the hell? I think. Why not? I'm still gonna get a day's pay. Might as well be sittin' in the shade pullin' a few coldies, right? So we sit and we drink. After a good four or five he lets it spill, the whole lot, even showed me the written report from his hired snoop. And, like you, I ask the obvious question: what you going to do about it?

"He was staring out at the busted up landscape, sort of solemn like, you know? 'You don't want to know,' he told me, and by the way he said it, I knew he was right about that. The quiet ones, right?

"It was about a year later I learned what happened. Old Casper paid me up there and then, even kicked in an extra five hundred, and I hitched out of that wild west town the following day.

" I was here in the city, at the Globe Hotel, downing a few one nothin' afternoon. There was this guy sitting on his own at the corner of the bar. That dude was knocking back whiskey like water, pissed as, but managing to stay propped on the bar stool, so they continued to serve what he asked for. And he muttering a bunch of really weird shit. Mostly unintelligible, but dark stuff, you know what I mean?

"I was playing pool with one of the regulars and I inquires as to the nature of this guy's problem. But not 'til the game was over did my opponent pull me aside and, quietly like, tell me what he knew. So now I'll give you the rest of the story as best I could gather from this guy's account, and from other sources besides.

"After I left Coober, old Casper set in motion this plan he had in all likelihood conceived way down in the shadowy passageways of the mine. He sent a telegram south, telling Tassie Pete he had struck it big. 'Mother lode. Come quick,' was reportedly the short but impelling message.

"Casper was waiting when he arrived back, and was apparently convincing in his role as one who after years of toil had finally unearthed his fortune. He laughed with delight at his partner's return. Lots of back- slapping and joshing and blokey stuff like that. But before the great discovery could be revealed, drinks were compulsory.

"From his own recounting, as passed on by another who claimed intimate association with the man, Tassie Pete had been extended one last opportunity to come clean about his transgression. While being plied with liquor, Casper esquires after his wife, and like, 'did you enjoy being back in the world?' And that's what I reckon, too. Fair dinkum. If the guy had owned up, said he was sorry, having gotten to know Casper as well as I did, I reckon things would have gone somewhat different. But he never had the guts to take the option. Cowardly bastard. But he'd had the option and missed his chance.

"So now Casper slips the mickey — a narcotic, sleepers or something — and old Pete wakes up sometime later to one hell of a nasty surprise.

"He came to in the tool-shed. The first thing he notices in his befuddled state is that he's laying on his back on bare ground, and that he's in his birthday suit. Naked as the day he was born. After that, things take a turn for the worse.

"The shed had been emptied. At its centre a steel drilling rod had been driven deep, with only a few inches left above ground. To this, a length of chain had been welded. At the end of the chain a padlock, hooked through the last link, and imagine his surprise! The padlock had been snugly snapped shut about his scrotum, his balls protruding like a pair of ripe plums. And there could be no mystery about the reason for his dire predicament. Casper left no room for that. Beside him lay the full written report made by the hired snoop, photographs included, and beneath this Tassie Pete's only hope of escape. . . a rusty and not very sharp cut-throat razor."

Morris sat silently waiting while Spider remained attentive and expectant, as if not quite sure the narrative had ended. A pained expression crept slowly across his face, tightening. Then a wince accompanied by a constricted groan deep in his throat, indicating to Morris that his friend had finally grasped the full implication. In fact, Spider was now looking decidedly pasty. "You don't look so good," Morris observed.

"Making a fellah cut off his own nuts? That's . . . sick!"

The note of outrage in Spider's voice took Morris aback. "Spider, the guy was an absolute arse-hole. People are killed for less, don't you know? You surprise me, buddy. I thought you'd appreciate the rough justice of it. I thought you dug that sort of thing."

"It was all true?" Spider asked irritably.

"Far as I can tell. Yeah, all true."

"The guy at the bar had no balls?"

"Tassie Pete. No balls. Correct."

Spider seemed unfathomably at a loss, unable to conceive the reality and searching the scenery as he grappled with the meaning of it.

Morris scratched his head in contemplation. "Spider! This is a perfect illustration of what can happen to someone if they cross the boundaries of acceptable human behaviour.

"He did a very bad thing. I'm not saying I agree with the punishment meted out, but retribution can come in various forms and in varying degrees of severity. Think it through. The way Casper had been treated. How he must'a felt."

"No," Spider protested. "Someone even thought to do a thing like that to me, I'd cut their guts out. I'd smash their fuckin' head to pulp!"

"What you gettin' so excited about?" Morris inquired calmly, a little concerned by Spider's manifest perturbation. "Jesus man. Why you ain't chuckling your fool head off like normal is beyond me.

"Because it ain't funny," Spider responded. "I ain't laughin' because it ain't funny, Morris! Why'd you go tellin' me such a sick story for anyway?"

Morris was nonplussed. After a moment staring at the flushed face before him, he sighed, slowly slipped off his boots. "Fuck it," he pronounced, standing, and taking possession of his beer, set off, making towards the water in long, easy strides.

Now suddenly alone, Spider watched from beneath the zodiac printed umbrella as Morris waded, fully clothed, into the Southern Ocean.

Upon reaching chest depth he halted and turned to face the shore with beer can in hand. He seemed prepared to stay there for some time. It was a beautiful summers day and he was determined to enjoy it.

UNFORESEEN CIRCUMSTANCES

AT 8:25 P.M., Morris and Spider locked the front door of number seven and crossed the lawn to where their van was parked in the driveway. Morris had exchanged his salt-stained jeans for another, less cruddy pair, and he had on his grey cotton work shirt, the sleeves rolled half-way up his forearms.

Spider wore black jeans and a t-shirt which oddly drew attention to his sunburned head, near glowing in the slanted evening light; and in mind of their pending engagement he had opted for a pair of wrap- around dark glasses.

Following a few steps behind him, Morris began to chuckle.

"What's funny?"

"Is that painful?"

"No."

"Looks painful."

"Well it's not."

They climbed into the van, slammed the doors closed and Morris slotted the key into the ignition.

"Remember years ago, that toy, Mr Potato-head? They went off the market. I think because there was the danger kids might choke on the bits. They had like detachable noses and ears and eyes and stuff. You could stick 'em on real fruit and veg."

"So?"

"He had a bunch of friends like Katie Carrot, Percy Parsnip and that sort of thing. A whole gang of 'em."

Spider kept his eyes straight ahead, not wanting to encourage Morris pursuing the topic any further. "Are we going to get going, or not?"

Morris leaned forward, reaching beneath his seat, and pulled out an old, beaten-up felt hat. He slapped it several times in order to beat off the dust, and passed it across.

"The shades are a nice touch," he said, "but the state of your noggin might not have quite the psychological effect we're looking for. Here, Mr Tomato-head ain't going to cut it. Serious."

Spider accepted the hat, placed it gingerly on top of his head. "Excellent" Morris pronounced. "Even if I didn't know you, you'd still scare me."

The address Madden had given them was virtually around the corner. Morris drove slowly through the back streets until they emerged at The Esplanade, near the top of the hill, and then turned left, hugging the curb as he counted down the house numbers.

"Fourteen!" Spider pointed out a two storey, grey brick house.

"Right," Morris replied, and continued on past.

At the bottom of the hill he made an illegal U-turn *(it pained Morris to do it. A copper issuing a ticket right now would blow the gaff, big-time, but they needed to stay on schedule)* and started back up the slope. Drawing level with the house, this time he pulled over to the curb and wrenched on the hand-brake.

A tall hedge bordered the front of the property but the driveway was wide and the gate wide open, affording a view of the carport on the right side, where a sparkling clean, black Porsche coupe was parked, and of most of the front of the house. There were few windows on the ground floor. Two bedrooms on the left, front door about centre, and what was probably a small lounge room to the right — curtains drawn on all. Upstairs had a wide balcony running along its whole length. Large plate-glass windows and a glass door leading out onto it. Again, all curtains were drawn. "Okay?" Morris asked. "Two exits, front door and balcony." Spider nodded and Morris pulled them away from the curb. He made two right turns and soon they were parked at the rear of the house. Here a tall timber paling fence proved a hindrance. At its centre, a pair of heavy gates secured with a chain, padlocked from within. Only the top storey of the house was visible. Again the lounge windows, and exposed plumbing indicated a toilet and bathroom to the right. Just above the height of the timber fence and close to it, the apex of a corrugated iron roof, probably only a storage shed of some kind.

"We'll walk in from the front then," Morris determined.

He parked at the top of the hill where the council had provided a parking bay near the cliff's edge, overlooking the sea. "Perfect. We'll hoof it in around twenty minutes," he advised. "Twilight makes it difficult for would-be witnesses to give descriptions.

They sat, silently watching as the sun descended beyond the brilliant horizon. High gold edged stratus cloud gradually became pink and lilac, the waiting moments strangely distorting, transmuting into something almost tangible as colours deepened and shifted through hews red to violet. After a good while Morris checked his wristwatch to find fifteen minutes had slipped silently by. The light was beginning to fade fast.

"What we going to do to this guy?" Spider asked.

"Hopefully, nothing at all except to convince him it's a very bad idea not to hand over Madden's bullshit investments. If he knows anything about Eddie, and why wouldn't he? he'd have to be pretty spooked already. Beats me why he'd do something like that and still be hangin' round. Damn curious, I'd say. If it was me I'd be out of state by now, at least. Getting on that bastard's wrong side is a decidedly stupid thing to do."

Spider pulled his cigarettes from his pocket and offered one to Morris, which was accepted silently. They lit up and smoked for a while.

"Did I ever tell you what they used to call Eddie a few years back?"

Spider shook his head.

"Nails," Morris told him. "You know how he got to be called that?"

"How?

"Some guy got in debt with him when he was first startin' out. I've known Eddie for yonks. His younger brother and I were mates at high school, but he's dead now, from an overdose. Anyway, Eddie went round to visit the guy and the guy says how he hasn't got the money just yet, like he always did, and just like Eddie expected. Eddie was surprisingly understanding. Said it was cool and would he like a *taste,* gratis, just to show there was no problem.

"The guy accepted, of course, and Eddie mixed him a blast that knocked him flat. Then while the guy was unconscious, Eddie nails his feet to the floor and splits. Nasty, eh? And he did it more than once! He nailed a guy's hands to a kitchen table, and another time, a woman's foot the wall. When I asked him he told me how it was good for business, and he certainly had bugger all overdue payments after word got around."

Spider whistled through his teeth. "Pretty smart, that."

"Smart? You're jokin'." The man's a fuckin' psycho. A boil on the butt of humanity. You remember that. Don't go thinking he's anything but a very nasty piece of work, got it?"

Spider didn't answer, which Morris knew was a less than positive indication. Clearly, he would have to broach the subject again and with greater perspicacity. At some future juncture, however. It was time to make a move.

"C'mon," he said, crushing out his cigarette in the ashtray. "Let's get this grubby little deed over with."

They locked the van and Morris stood regarding the driver's side window in annoyance: still jammed half-way and no handle to budge it. "Bugger it," he pronounced, and off down the hill they began.

As they neared the house they noticed, through gaps in the curtains, that the top room was lit. Just ahead of them rusty hinges squeaked and an elderly lady appeared from behind an obscuring oleander, a small dog at the end of a leash.

Passing close by her was unavoidable. Spider lowered his head and Morris raised his hand to his face, as if to scratch an eyebrow.

"Good evening," the old lady piped cheerfully, dentures almost dislodging with a strenuous smile.

Both mumbled an inarticulate reply.

"I say," she called as they passed. "Excuse me!"

Morris was compelled to halt, not wanting them to be remembered as suspicious, ill-mannered types.

"Yeah?" - his hand still at his face.

"I'm afraid I missed the weather tonight. Frodo was making such a terrible ruckus in the yard, I had to go out and investigate. He was telling the neighbour's cat off for coming over the fence. He's very territorial. Yorkie's are, you know. Can you tell me what tomorrow's forecast is? Do you know?"

"Same as today," Morris said in a very low voice.

"Oh dear, what a shame. I do so dislike this heat. My asthma, you know. Difficulty breathing. Oh well, thank-you so much. Have a nice evening, both of you. Come on, Frodo. Let's have a nice walk to Aunty Ethel's."

Morris groaned. "Off to a terrific start." And just as they reached the driveway Eddie Madden drove past in his white Ford LTD. Passing under the carport on the right side of the house, they moved to the rear. Spider peeked around the corner to check that the coast was clear and they continued silently on to the back door. Morris climbed the three concrete steps to peer in through the window. "Can see through to the front room. No one down here. Light shining down the staircase."

He tried the door. It opened silently.

"Just a moment," he said as Spider stepped up behind him, and from his back pocket he pulled out a bandanna which he tied, cowboy fashion, about his face. "Okay."

Three steps into the kitchen music started up from the top room, causing Morris to stop and Spider to bump into him. They moved to the foot of the stairs and started up, cautiously, the fifth step creaking under their combined weight, fortunately lost to the strains of Ella Fitzgerald wailing soulfully above.

At the top a railing edged three sides of the stairwell, and against these rested two bookcases and a high-backed couch. Lilac curtains covering the rear windows were Morris's only view at the head of the stairs.

When Spider crawled up beside him, his eyes as wide as saucers, Morris stood up slowly, taking in as much of the room at once as he could.

On the couch, a man facing away from him, only the back of his head visible. The room was a clutter with books, record albums and an assortment of musical instruments. A large cabinet against one wall housed hi-fi equipment and hundreds of CD's. At the opposite wall, a red cedar table and chair, the table stacked high with books and papers.

"Okay," Morris whispered. "Let's do it."

Miles Owen sat at the middle of the couch, slumped forward, a glass of red wine in his hands and a bottle at his feet. He was clad only in a red bathrobe. He wore gold-rimmed spectacles and his light-brown hair was cut short, combed forward without a parting. He looked to be a young man, around thirty-five, his face lightly tanned, round and fresh-looking as though he took special care, using moisturiser and such - a man who pampered himself.

The sudden appearance of uninvited strangers either side of him, one wearing a felt hat and sunglasses, the other a red bandanna over his face, caused him to start. His light-blue eyes flickered in rapid evaluation, and without making any sudden move, he said, "I don't have much that would interest you. There's two hundred dollars in my wallet. Take it and go. I won't even bother phoning the police."

Morris ignored this and motioned for Spider to shut off the music. When he had done so, he replied, "That's very kind of you, Miles, but we're not here to rob you. It is Miles, isn't it? Miles Owen?"

When Owen failed to answer, Morris assumed he had the right man. "We're not here for any terrible purpose, either, Mr Owen. Don't look so worried."

Owen seemed to find little comfort in this, and continued to be frightened.

"I'll get straight to the point," Morris continued. "But, no, perhaps you can tell *me* why we're here, eh? Can you guess?" Owen's brow furrowed for a moment. He shook his head. "No."

"Oh dear. That's too bad. You'd think that a man would remember taking something that doesn't belong to him."

Morris stooped and lifted up the bottle of wine. "Can't be the claret affecting your memory. Not unless this isn't your first bottle."

"Tell me what you want," Owen said, plucking up some courage. "When I'm being intimidated in my own home, I like to know for what reason."

"Guess," Morris insisted.

"I don't know," Owen immediately answered.

"Is that because you've been a bit naughtier than usual this month? Can't hazard a guess? Alright then." To Spider he said, "Would you be kind enough to tell the man why we've come to visit?"

Spider had taken an interest in the record collection stacked in the shelves against the wall. He was caught napping. "Eh? Oh, yeah. You got Eddie's stuff ... bonds or something."

Morris turned back to Owen. "Startin' to come back to you now?" Owen seemed at a loss. "Bonds? Eddie? You don't mean Eddie Madden?"

Morris nodded. "Very good. Now, let's stop friggin' around. Give us the bonds and we're out of here, no drama." He tapped the wine bottle lightly against his leg. "I hope you're a better accountant than you are a crook, because you show no aptitude for it. In fact, it was downright stupid of you to try it on with Eddie."

Owen's expression went blank. He raised his hands, palms upward, and began to shake his head. "Look, fellahs, I don't know what to say. I don't like be contradictive, but you appear to be operating under some kind of misapprehension. I worked for Eddie Madden in a professional capacity for just over one year. That association has ceased, and as-"

"Shut it!" Morris ordered, and Owen obeyed. "Don't give me this shit, Miles. I don't need it. Now, the next time you open your mouth you are going to tell me the whereabouts of Madden's precious bloody bonds. We will then take possession, we will leave and there will be no grief, okay?"

Fear was now obvious in Owen's eyes. Again he raised upturned palms, but he kept his mouth pressed shut.

Morris saw that he was running out of options. "Damn you, man," he growled angrily." He kicked Owen in frustration, the toe of his heavy boot striking Owen on the shin and producing a sharp cry of pain. "Don't keep this up," he warned.

Owen was doubled over, holding the battered leg while Morris watched on, shaking his head. "Look what you made me do," he complained, and took to pacing while Owen continued to nurse the painful injury.

"Why don't we look for them?" Spider offered.

"Yeah, right," Morris agreed, trying not to sound too ashamed for having overlooked the obvious alternative. "We'll have to tie him up. Can't watch him and search at the same time."

"Help, police!" Owen screamed. "Help! Help! Hel..!" Spider covered the intervening distance quickly, clamped his hand over Owen's mouth and wrestled him to the floor.

While the two grappled frantically on the carpet, Morris rifled the draws beside the cedar table until he discovered a roll of masking tape.

Spider had Owen pinned down by the time Morris arrived to assist. "You damned idiot," he hissed, and set about binding and gagging his hostage.

For the next thirty minutes the pair searched the house from top to bottom, and came up with nothing. They returned to the upstairs room where Owen lay bound and helpless on the couch. Morris dragged him upright.

"Alright, mister, where's the safe? And don't bother denying there is one."

Owen mumbled something incomprehensible through the tape. "Oh, yeah." Morris tore away the tape from his mouth. "What was that again?"

"It's in the spare room." He motioned towards the doorway to the right. "Inside the cupboard."

"Good. Let's go."

Owen had to be freed from his bindings before being escorted into the adjoining room. There he opened the in-built wardrobe, and at the back of it slid aside a panel to reveal the safe.

"Open it," Spider prompted, and Owen compliantly set to work on the combination lock, in short time straightening himself and snapping back the lock.

Spider stepped forward and swung open the door. On the shelves sat a lot of papers and bound documents. Some cash, too, mostly hundred dollar and fifty dollar notes bound into wads.

Spider whistled through his teeth. "We're rich," he chirped. "No we're not," Morris replied. "We agreed, no freelancing."

Spider turned to face his partner, his face displaying an array of emotions in quick succession, incredulity taking precedence. "You're joking," he finally responded.

"Take Owen back to the couch. I'll be in shortly." "I never agreed," Spider said obstinately.

"If you had a problem with the arrangement, Spider, you had the opportunity to say so at the time. We accepted the terms offered.

And you!" He turned to Owen. "You had better start being a little more helpful. I'm getting thoroughly pissed off with this whole deal."

Spider decided to let drop the matter of the money for the time being. Morris was hard to talk to when he was upset. He led his hostage into the other room while Morris made an inspection of the safe's contents, cursing and muttering as he did so.

"You oughtn't to make him mad," Spider warned, sitting Owen on the couch. "He once cut a guy's balls off."

Owen neither replied nor appeared at all concerned. A look of fatalism had come over his face. He sat quietly with thoughts seemingly elsewhere.

After a few minutes Morris struggled in with the pile of folders and papers. Halting before Owen and Spider, he let the load fall to the floor.

"I can't find anything in this pile of shit. Is it here?" he demanded. Owen looked up dolefully. "I need a drink," he said. "Give me a drink and I'll tell you."

"A drink?" Morris looked around the room. "A drink. Sure. The man want's a drink. Why not?"

He stalked across the room to where an imperial pint glass sat at the corner of a shelf. Returning with it, he poured the remaining claret into it and held it out for Owen to take.

"Thank-you," he said, taking possession, and while Morris and Spider watched with mounting interest, the subdued accountant drank his way to the bottom of the glass.

"Now," said Morris. "Where is it?"

Owen held the empty glass up between thumb and forefinger, observing Morris's distorted image through it. He let it drop to the carpet and followed its progress as it rolled away.

Morris swung his boot at it, sending it flying into the corner of the room where it bounced to a standstill.

Owen looked up from his vulnerable position to the looming Morris, then turned to Spider beside him. "Spider ..." He looked again to Morris. ".. Whoever you are. This document of which you speak. This bank bond or whatever. I know not of its whereabouts, nor do I have the faintest interest."

Morris was astounded. But even if he could have summoned a suitable response, it would have had to wait. The telephone on Owen's desk broke the silence with a shrillness which made Morris flinch.

"Blast!" he hissed vehemently, and turned to Spider. "No prizes for guessing who that'll be."

He strode angrily across the room to the desk, lifted the receiver and grunted into the mouthpiece.

Madden: "Morris, have you recovered my property?

Morris: "Not yet."

Madden: "You're taking your time. Thought I could depend on you."

Morris: "I'm taking care of it. Don't sweat."

Madden: "I told you the man is a practised bullshit artist. As slippery as an eel. Don't let him play you for a sucker. People like him think they're superior, with their private school education and their well-paid, cushy jobs and all. Don't let him make a mug out of you, Morris. You're five times the man he is. Teach him some respect. I'll call back ."

Morris replaced the receiver and turned to eye his quarry. "That was him, was it?" Owen sneered. "The big cheese giving instructions to his little cheeses. Well, what's the word? A bit of the old biffo, is it? Cement shoes? Well, to hell with it, I don't care, you hear? I don't care."

Owen lolled forward, burying his face in his hands, and as he began to sob Morris looked questioningly to Spider. "What the hell's the matter with him?"

Spider shrugged."Said he had heartburn." "What?"

"Yeah, heartburn. Got the pills in his pocket."

Morris stepped over and searched the pockets of his bathrobe, finding the pill-bottle in question.

"Serenace," he read from the label. "Bloody antidepressants, and a pint of plonk to boot.

"Shut up that infernal snivelling! Give me what I want or its location, and we're out of your life. Or don't, in which case I think I'm going to toss you head first off that balcony." He jabbed a thumb in the general direction.

"I don't care. Do it," he sobbed. "My life isn't worth living."

Morris rolled his eyes to the ceiling. "Oh, Christ. We've got a depressed, suicidal basket-case on our hands." He was about to step away, but propped. "Or have we?

"This some sort of smart-arse act you putting on?" "Ooooooooo," Owen mocked, and broke into insipid laughter."Are you going to hurt me some more? Because if you are it still won't get you what you want. Nothing will. I don't have it. I don't have anything." He fell to sobbing once more.

Morris's face expressed bemusement. With a nod of the head he signalled Spider and the two moved across the room to confer.

"Do you think he's faking?" Morris asked, "Madden says he's a bit of a clever bastard."

"Possible," Spider answered, shrugging. "Don't think so though.

Why don't we just knock him around for a while and see what gives?"

"I don't know," Morris demurred. "I'm not sure he warrants a slapping. I don't like to. Let's play good-guy, bad-guy."

"Only if I get to be bad-guy," Spider replied.

They returned to stand before the couch where Owen sat doubled over and staring at his feet in blank despondency.

Spider said, "Let me go to work on him. He knows alright. The bastard is just jerkin' us around."

Owen did not respond.

"No, let's give him a chance. He's obviously not well. Violence should be the last resort."

"You goin' soft or somethin'? Try it your way then, and when that fails I'm gonna start cuttin' off bits. That always works."

Owen groaned but still would not look up. "Back off for a while," Morris said. "I want to talk to him, try and convince him it ain't worth what he's putting himself through."

"Okay, but then he's mine, right?"

Spider backed up a step, waited a moment for effect. "I once read about these tribes somewhere, how they were into cutting off ears and things from their enemies." He turned and walked away.

"He likes that sort of thing." Morris told Owen. "Watched too much crap on TV when he was a kid, I reckon. Television, eh? Not surprising there's so many fucked up kids around these days."

He squatted beside Owen in order to get his attention. "Miles, what's the matter with you? It doesn't have to be this way. You don't even pay heed. I'm trying to help you. Talk to me, man. What's got you so screwed up you don't care if my buddy starts workin' on you?"

Owen raised his eyes. "Masked man come to help Miles?"

Morris sighed heavily. Even in his present condition Owen had seen through the hackneyed ploy. "Yeah, not terribly original, is it," he admitted, and slipped the bandanna off over his head. "There. No more bullshit, okay?"

Owen chuckled. "You looked better with it on."

"Look," said Morris. "Let me clarify the situation and help you make a rational decision here. You have something we want, and, Miles, let me point out this little technicality to you, that something does not belong to you. The deal I offer you is very generous. Give back what you took and we are not required to take any further action. You must admit, it's really a very good offer."

Owen let himself fall back into the couch, groaning pathetically. "Oh, Gloria. Why?"

"Oh dear," said Morris, suddenly enlightened. "So that's it. You've got woman problems?"

Owen became maudlin again. "She's gone," he expressed tearfully. "I should have known it was too good to be true. Why would a beautiful woman want to be with someone like me?" He gritted his teeth. "I'll tell you why. To use me, that's why. Use me up and toss me aside like so much . . . like so much. . . ?"

"Toilet paper?" Morris offered.

Owen sobered a little. "That's a bit strong, isn't it?" "Is it? Sorry."

Owen sniffed back his tears. "It's okay. I guess it's fairly close to the truth anyway."

"You were in love with her then?"

He nodded glumly. "Yeah. What a schmuck, eh?"

"What do you mean? It happens. Anyone can fall in love." He regarded Spider for a moment. He was presently occupied with searching through a waste-paper basket beside the desk. "Well, almost anybody, I expect."

"But unrequited love! I feel so foolish. She took my cheque-book, my credit cards!"

"What a bitch. I hope you cancelled them. Hey, what'd you say her name was again?"

"Gloria. Gloria Fenwick."

"Now there's a coincidence. Mad Eddie's piece is called Gloria." "That's right. That's her."

Morris's eyes grew wide in amazement. "Miles, you crazy bastard. Are you tellin' me you been messin' with Eddie Madden's woman?"

Owen nodded sheepishly.

"Did you hear that, Spider?"

"I sure did. You'll be lucky if he doesn't cut your balls off."

"Does he know?" Morris asked. "Not that I know of."

"Miles, tell me straight, I implore you. This is very important. What do you know about this missing bank bond?"

Owen looked Morris unwaveringly in the eye. "That's just what I keep trying to tell you. I know nothing of any bonds. Really, nothing at all!" "Goddamnit," Morris whispered hoarsely. "You know, I think I actually believe you. That *bitch*, Gloria. I bet it was her, judging by the way she fleeced you too."

"Hey, don't talk about her like that. Where do you get off calling her a bitch!"

Owen tried too quickly to stand and challenge Morris. He overbalanced in getting to his feet and Morris had to push him back into his seat.

"Cool it, Miles, before you hurt yourself. What the hell you doin' defending her honour after the way she treated you? Where's your self-respect, man?"

Owen began to sob again and Morris called Spider over. "You been catchin' most of this?"

"Yeah, most," Spider replied.

"So what do you think, this Gloria chick swiped the goods?" "Sure does look that way."

"Yeah," said Morris, thoughtfully. "Sure looks that way to me too."

An interval of restful inactivity fell on the trio for a short time, during which Owen's weeping ebbed to silence. The hush was then shattered by the trill of the telephone.

Morris remained where he stood, exhibiting a mien of deep contemplation until his attention broke from the lamenting creature before him. At last, he turned and crossed unhurriedly to the persistent source of annoyance.

Morris: "Yeah." Madden: "Well?" Morris: "Nah." (silence)

Madden: "You work him over?" Morris: "Plenty."

Madden:"Good ... Now snuff him."

Morris: "What? No way, uh-uh. Are you nuts?"

Madden: "Listen, and listen good. You don't do this and your arse is history, understand? And as an added incentive, I have deposited twenty- five grams of good quality hammer in the tea canister on your kitchen shelf. That's yours. A bonus on top of what we already agreed. However, if I don't have proof of that little worm's demise within the next thirty minutes I can guarantee the coppers will be kicking in your front door in thirty-five. Savvy?"

(Silence)

Madden: "Well, got to go now. You'll be hearing from me. Oh, and one thing more. There's a package on the back step for you."

Madden hung up.

"Spider, check out if there's anything at the back door, would you?" While Spider went to look, Morris began pacing the floor.

"Something wrong?" Owen asked.

Morris answered without turning to his hostage. "You could say that. Just give me a couple of minutes, alright?"

Owen clammed up, sensing that something serious was in the wind, and when Spider came bounding back up the stairs with a small package wrapped in brown paper, he silently indicated that Morris was not to be disturbed.

Spider seated himself beside Owen and waited, the package balanced on his knees. He gave it an experimental shake which revealed nothing. Curiosity tempted, but now he dare not act without his friend's say so: he, too, sensed something untoward brewing.

Morris ceased his pacing and positioned himself in a chair where he could address the others. "It's a present from Madden. Open it," he told Spider.

Spider pulled a pocket-knife from his jeans pocket, opened it and cut neatly along the top of the parcel. Folding back the paper, a look of wonder appeared on his face. He reached in and pulled out a black .38 revolver.

Owen made a squeaking noise in the back of his throat.

"It's alright, Miles," Morris reassured. "This type of caper is way out of my field." He paused, allowing Owen time to consider this. "Are you able to think clearly?" he added, unsure of Owen's present mental state.

"I think so," came the somewhat unconvincing reply.

At least he wasn't going to pieces, Morris observed with some relief. He noticed Spider playing with the gun; on the verge of cocking back the hammer.

"For Christ's sake, put that thing down before you hurt someone!" Spider put it quickly down on the couch between himself and Owen. Owen picked it up just as quickly and leapt up, side-stepping from the couch to bring the two intruders into a manageable field of fire.

"That wasn't the brightest thing I've ever seen you do," Morris commented.

"You told me to put it down," Spider replied lamely. "Yeah, but Jesus, man. It should have occurred to you-"

"Shut up!" Owen intervened, holding the gun two-handed at chest height and looking entirely incompetent.

"No, look, Miles," Morris insisted. "I'm sorry but this is important. My friend here just put a loaded weapon down beside a man under the impression he was still under threat. I'm not impressed, and I think he should be taken to task over the issue. The ramifications... Firstly, Spider, you have put Miles in a position whereby he might cause actual bodily harm to another human being. I think you should apologise, don't you?"

Miles appeared stunned. Morris folded his arms and waited for Spider. "I'm sorry," Spider obliged. "Really, I am. Morris is quite right, I wasn't thinking ."

"Good," said Morris. "Now, secondly and more importantly is the fact that, due to certain unforeseen circumstances, the entire complexion of this, ah. . . shall we say, gathering? has been radically altered."

"If you don't get out of my house, immediately, I'll shoot!" Owen steadied his aim in Morris's direction.

"And my next point covers that," Morris explained anxiously. "You see, we're not the bad guys any more. You're not the thief and we're not the bad guys. And, you see, we can't leave now because-"

Owen fired the gun.

With the explosion Spider bolted for the windows, evidently intending to crash through the glass and escape via the balcony. The drawn curtains, however, made this a chancy endeavour, and striking the door-frame at pace, he slammed to an instantaneous halt and crumpled to the floor.

Also on the floor was Morris, looking up at Owen who still had the gun pointed in his general direction.

"Shit, Miles. You scared the bejesus outa me." "Sorry," Owen replied instinctively.

"That's okay. You're scared. And I guess what with the wine and the pills and all... Well, no harm done, eh?"

Spider moaned. He lay flat on his back beside the curtains.

"Listen, Miles, we'll go if you say so, but only after you hear me out. I can't say fairer. The fact is, if we leave like this all our arses are, to borrow a phrase, history. Fact is, I'd rather be shot by you than by Eddie bloody Madden."

Owen was thoughtful for a time, the end result being a puzzled expression. "What the fuck is going on?" he demanded, exasperation telling in his voice.

"Can I go help my friend, Miles? I'll just get him to the couch. We'll both sit there and you can sit here." He indicated a spot in front of the couch. "Drag that wooden chair over and keep us covered, okay? Then I'll fill you in on everything."

"I don't know. Maybe. I suppose that would be alright. But no sudden moves though, or I'll let you have it."

"I don't doubt that. Hey, you okay? You look a bit pale."

"I'm just fine. Pick up your buddy and lets get -" Owen failed to finish. His knees buckled and he went down in a dead faint.

"Unbelievable," Morris muttered to himself, looking about him. "I've never in all my born days. . . What a dogs breakfast!"

He went to Owen first, picked up the gun and emptied out the rounds, pushing them into his pocket. The gun he replaced in Owen's hand. Then to Spider, who was beginning to come around. He helped him to stand and guided him carefully to the couch. When he was seated, he asked, "You going to be alright?"

"Yeah, no worries. Hey, I thought you was shot."

"I hope you're not too put out. Say, that was some stunning display of heroism. Never knew you could move so fast."

Spider offered a wry smile. "Was quite the athlete, once."

Owen stirred. Morris spoke quickly and quietly. "I've emptied the gun.

I want to gain his confidence, so play along."

Spider nodded. "Ouch! That hurts." He raised his hand to a fast- swelling lump at the centre of his forehead.

Morris looked at it closely. "Ooo, that's a beaut."

"Stay where you are!" Owen pushed himself up with one arm, his free hand holding the gun, waveringly.

"Sure, no worries," Morris and Spider chorused. "What happened?"

"You nearly killed Morris," Spider answered irritably.

"Sorry, Morris. I didn't really mean for it to go off. Boy, that is some lump on your head," he told Spider.

Owen climbed to his feet and dragged a chair over in front of the couch. "Where were we?"

"Exactly," Morris said. "Time is limited. I think I know what is happening here and there may just be a solution."

Before he could continue, he was interrupted by the telephone. "I've got to answer that, Miles."

Owen merely shrugged, but tightened his grip on the gun.

"Good," said Morris, rising and heading for the telephone. "The gunshot, that was good. That was very, very good, Miles. We can work with that."

He lifted the receiver: "Eddie?"

Madden: "We heard the shot. Was that it?" Morris: "It's done."

Madden: "That's just fine, Morris. I'm impressed. Of course I'll need to see the proof."

Morris: "Naturally. I knew that. You coming up?" (Heart in mouth)

Spider and Owen exchanged looks of trepidation.

Madden: "You think I'm stupid? No, of course I'm not coming up. Take it to your place. I'll see you there."

Morris: "Yeah. . . um, look, there's a bit of a mess here. The shot didn't finish him right off. Had to finish it with a" - he spotted a didgeridoo mounted on the wall - "didgeridoo. The gun makes too much noise so we're gonna have to clean up a bit. Fingerprints and all that forensic shit, right?"

Madden: " Your place in an hour." He hung up.

"Okay, good," Morris said to the attentive pair on the couch. "We've got an hour to decide what we're going to do."

"We?" Owen objected.

Spider gave him one of his dirty looks—looks he secretly practiced in the bathroom mirror when no one was around. "Ya know how Eddie got his name?"

"I assume his parents thought Edward was a good name,"

"No, not Edward... *Nails!* He's called Nails because he used to nail people to stuff. Walls, tables and like that."

"Oh, I see," said Owen, disinterested and wondering at the relevancy. "So?"

"So, you're still in deep shit. Eddie finds you ain't dead, you soon will be. Us too maybe. Lucky Morris has got a plan, eh, Morris." Morris showed some annoyance. "I said we had an hour, not a flamin' week. But Spider's right. Your arse is in a sling, *boyo*, and without your participation we're sunk."

"Why don't we just run?" Owen tried.

"You ready to lose all this, Miles? Your job, your house, your way of life and whatever friends you have? More importantly, your self-respect!

Are you going to throw in your hand because of one jumped-up, self-important, bloodsucking, stand-over merchant like Madden?"

"Well, if it-"

"Of course not," Morris continued. "No man worth his salt would allow such a personal affront. The mere thought is enough to curdle a man's blood. Ain't that right, Spider!"

"That's right."

"You're damned right it's right. Right, Miles?" "I guess so," he replied .

"Right, then it's agreed. We steel our resolve and act with courage." For Owen's benefit he adopted a pose meant to instill resolve.

"Would you mind very much explaining what's going on?"

"Good, Miles. A positive contribution. Perhaps you'd like drop of wine?" Owen cheered slightly. "Well, I wouldn't mind."

"Spider, would you play mother?" He gave a wink as he said this; barely discernible but his eyes plainly conveyed his meaning.

In short time Spider returned from downstairs with a glass and two bottles of wine.

Morris waited until the glass was filled and Owen had taken a slaking good draught before regaining his attention.

"Now. To answer your question, Miles. I find I have to work on the premise that you are telling the truth, knowing Madden as well as I do. He really is a devious bastard.

"We accepted this undertaking having been led to believe it involved no more than the recovery of stolen property. You, the said perpetrator, I had never met, but Madden imparted no sense of doubt as to your being guilty, warning us that you would plead your innocence to the last. We were to retrieve his property, whatever it took, inferring we were to beat it out of you. That much is straightforward enough. The return of his property was paramount.

"And then, despite the fact that we hadn't yet achieved our objective, but believing we had already given you a thorough going over, he instructs us to kill you. A sudden shift in priority. We do that and he does his dough. . . He's not like that! He doesn't call it quits until he gets what he's after. I'm forced, therefore, to consider that this precious stolen bank bond is a red herring.

"So then there is the little matter of your involvement with Gloria, and *bingo!* it all falls into place. I don't know about this bank bond thing. Maybe it exists and maybe it doesn't. Maybe it was Gloria who stole it, like she stole from you, then used you just long enough to get clear. It's irrelevant.

"What's not irrelevant is that he wants you dead. Why does he want you dead? Because you've been messin' with his woman. He knows, Miles. Think about it. A man like that sees everything either as a possession or a possible possession, and he knows the whereabouts of all his possessions at any time of the day or night, as a matter of course. If not, he gets crazy. Crazier still if he thinks he's been betrayed or made a fool of.

"As a result, Spider and myself get shafted. He concocted the story of the bonds, used the stolen bonds as an excuse to get us here. A while ago he threatened to frame us as drug peddlers and to have my house raided if we didn't comply with his insane instructions. The bastard had us in a corner."

"Had?" Owen questioned.

"Yes, *had*," Morris repeated. He noticed with some satisfaction that Owen's eyes were becoming glassy. "Your pot-shot, Miles. Remember? He thinks you're dead. Well, he thinks you might be dead."

"*Might* be?" Owens eyes widened fractionally.

Morris took a breath. "Okay. Look, here's the thing. He insists on viewing the corpse. Have a drink, Miles, you look a bit shaky."

"He wants to see *my corpse!*" Owen took Morris's advice and gulped down more wine.

A BEER WITH FRIENDS

AT AROUND TEN-THIRTY, Morris pulled the van up in his driveway and turned off the engine. Spider climbed out and went to open the front door while Morris checked that the street was clear before opening the side door of the van. With a heave, he lifted out a large roll of rug, grunting as he balanced it on one shoulder, and quietly slid shut the door. Spider passed through the front room and passageway to the kitchen before switching on a light, and there began to clear off the kitchen table by transferring everything on it to the top of the fridge. Hearing the front door slam closed he swept his arm across the table-top and stepped back out of the way. Morris strode in and dumped the roll on the table. "Check the tea canister," he said, turning. "Let's see if Madden was bluffing. No sign of a break-in, unless they came in through one of the back rooms."

When Spider lifted the lid off of the canister, surprise registered on his face. "Hey. Since when have we ever had tea in this thing?"

"What?" Morris stepped over and Spider tilted it towards him to see inside. It was full to the brim with tea-leaves.

"Let's see," Morris said, taking possession, and he turned it upside down over the sink, exposing what must have been twenty five one gram packets of heroin.

"Look at that!" Spider piped up gleefully. "Shit. He wasn't bluffing. I didn't think so, but ...

"Let's have a taste," Spider suggested.

"Okay. I'm about to keel over, myself. Better hurry though, he'll be here pretty soon."

The required utensils were laid out speedily. Water was boiled, syringes sterilized, and portions mixed to be drawn up through a cigarette filter. When they each had injected themselves, everything was gathered up to be either stored in its place or discarded in the kitchen waste bin.

Morris lit a cigarette and pushed himself up to sit on the bench-top beside the sink. Spider slumped in a chair beside the table, looking tired.

"I'm knackered," he said, sounding it. "I'm sunburnt, I've been knocked unconscious and I'm tired. And I'm hungry. God, I'm hungry. What we got in the fridge?"

"Bugger all. Hang on." Morris leaned across to open the cupboard on his left, and reaching in pulled out a cracker box. He gave it a shake. "You're in luck. Have a go at these," he said, tossing the box over to Spider.

Morris sat, smoking, watching as Spider devoured the last morsel of food in the house. When he had finished, Spider dropped the empty box and smacked his lips. "I shouldn't have done that. Now I'm really hungry."

Morris smiled. "Yeah, I know. A couple of glasses of water works better. How about we get a pizza after all this is over?"

Spider was about to reply but was cut short by a knock at the front door.

"Okay," said Morris, wearily lowering himself from the top of the bench. "Here we go."

Morris opened the front door and let Madden through. He held the door open longer, expecting another, stepped out to find no one about and came back in.

"Where's your five-eight?"

"On an errand," Madden answered amid darkness. "You guys tryin' to save power or something?"

"We're in the kitchen," Morris said, stepping by and leading him through.

Spider was standing near the sink when the two entered. Madden ignored him, his attention focused on the rolled up rug on the table. "He in there?"

"Yeah." Morris squeezed past, went to the end of the rug nearest the corner. "Made a bit of a mess of him. Some blokes have skulls like concrete." He folded back the end of the rug to allow Madden a view. "Miles ain't one of them."

Madden took a close look. The right side of the head was a mess of red goo, which also oozed from the ear and both nostrils. Partially dried, it had caked here and there, in the orbit of one eye and down his neck and had soaked the left shoulder of his bathrobe. Madden grunted with satisfaction and looked up to Morris. "Good job. Did he squeal much?"

"Are you kidding? Like a stuck pig," Morris told him. "It's curious, though. He never did tell us what he did with your dough. I'd have bet money on him spillin' his guts."

"Forget it," Madden said, bruskly, but then appeared to decide some further comment was necessary. "He gambled you wouldn't kill him. Probably expected to get out of it with a few bruises, maybe a busted leg. It would have been worth it for fifty grand." He flipped the rug back over Owen's face. "One less maggot in the world," he said dismissively, and turned to Spider.

"Good job, Spider. "You've shown more dash than I gave you credit for." He peered closely at Spider. "That sure is some sort of lump on your head, ain't it?" He chuckled, much amused. "What happened, walk into a door?"

Madden continued grinning at him for a while, then shook his head ruefully. "Alright, I guess it's squaring up time."

He reached into his hip pocket and withdrew his wallet, flipped it open to reveal a tightly packed wad of hundred-dollar notes in the fold. Of these he counted out two and handed them to Morris.

"What's this? You said, a five spot apiece!"

"On delivery of my property," Madden replied, coolly. "You got it?" Morris mreained q uiet.

Madden straightened himself to his full height. His voice was edged with rising animosity. "You accusing me of ripping you off?"

"I don't suppose." Morris conceded. "You're right. Five hundred apiece on delivery," he quoted.

"And the twenty-five grams for stiffing Owen, which I see you've already sampled."

Morris hated this, but technically Madden was quite right and he had no good argument to offer. "Sweet," he confirmed. "It's a done deal." "Alright," said Madden, forcibly calming himself. "The two hundred is purely for your time. You guys drew a blank. So bad luck. But do you see me spitting the dummy over *my* lost money? No you don't. And your debt of twelve, hundred. What's to stop me demanding that?"

Again Morris remained silent. He was having his nose rubbed in it and there was nothing he could do. This was Eddie Madden's thing. Have people perpetually indebted to you and start pulling their strings. . . and he was well practised at it.

Madden pulled his cigarettes from his pocket and lit one up. "But you're okay, Morris. You're reliable. The debt is wiped," he said with a magnanimous wave of the hand, and he turned his attention back to Spider. "I hope you're bright enough to understand how fortunate you are. That anyone would take you under their wing is fortune enough, but this guy? Huh." He jabbed his cigarette towards Spider. "If only a fraction rubs off, you'll be doing okay."

Spider nodded his head agreeably. "You're right. I will," he replied.

Madden giggled. "Will what, Spider?" And when Spider produced a confused look, he laughed out loud. "You fucking crack me up, Spider. You really do. Have you got any brothers as weird as you? I could use having someone around with as much amusement value."

Spider's expression became unreadable.

"Spider's one of a kind," Morris intervened. "Best partner I've ever had."

"Come off it, Morris. "You were always a loner before he happened along."

"We're a good team," Morris persisted. "Couldn't operate without him."

Madden let it go, glanced at his watch.

"Well, I suppose we had better dispose of the body," said Morris, hoping to precipitate Madden's departure.

"Not yet. I'm waiting for Lokki to arrive. Shouldn't be much longer." "Oh." Morris tried to disguise his disappointment. "Shall we repair to the lounge then?"

Morris led the way, flicking on the light switch as he entered the front room. Madden went to sit in the same corner chair had occupied earlier that day.

"You move your goods?" he asked.

"McCleary took the lot." Morris replied from beside the stereo, where he stood idly thumbing through his record albums.

"That's good. How much did he give you?" "Five hundred." Madden nodded. "About what I thought. You know you're being screwed?"

Morris let the records alone and reached to his shirt pocket for his cigarettes. "Not really." He tossed one across to Spider on the couch. "At least no more than anybody else.

"The government screws the workers, pensioners and retirees. I screw the well off. People like McLeary screw people like me. Bent coppers screw bent pawnbrokers like McLeary. Everyone screwing somebody, as I see it."

"No one screwing me over," Madden argued. Morris levelled his gaze towards him. "No?"

"I'm not saying it hasn't been tried," he conceded. "But trying isn't succeeding, and that's the big difference. People like Owen, for instance."

Morris deliberated for a moment, then said, "Miles didn't steal from you, but you knew that already, didn't you."

"Oh, but he did, Morris, and I assume you know what I mean. You must have learned a lot during the course of the evening," he said, now adopting something slightly less than a purely conversational tone. "I've been waiting with some expectancy to ask you what you make of it all. What have you surmised, Morris?"

"I'll need the answer to one small question before I could hazard a guess."

Madden smiled. "Alright. Go on then." "Is there actually a missing bank bond?"

A laugh of pure pleasure escaped Madden. "You never disappoint me, Morris. You never do. If you hadn't asked,

I'd have been very surprised. The answer is, yes, there most certainly is. So, now what do you say?"

"I'd say Gloria relieved you of it."

"But Miles would've had to be in on it, don't you think so?" Madden asked earnestly.

"I'd say not. I'm sure he would have spilled it if he had."

"Hmm," Madden expressed in consideration. "Not exactly how I'd figured it. Guess I'll have to trust your judgment on that. Still, he was far from being innocent, you must agree."

"We're all that," Morris answered. "But for any treacherous woman, poor old Miles had sucker written all over him."

"He paid the price of stupidity," Madden said, sharply. "As any stupid creature pays in life. Don't tell me you feel pity for him. You're too soft, Morris. That's your one, major flaw. If you weren't soft you'd be living in luxury like me, in stead of..." He hesitated. "Well, in stead of living like this. I can't fathom it. I don't understand you at all."

Morris shrugged. "I admit it ain't the Ritz, but what the hell do I care?

This whole neighbourhood is a shit-heap anyway."

"You can do better," Madden pushed. "I could help you."

Your kind of help I can do without, Morris thought. He remembered his daydream of that afternoon: an honest job, the respect of work-mates and friends in a small, rural community. If he thought Madden could possibly understand something so ordinary, he would have mentioned it.

"I like to do for myself," he said in reply.

Headlights reflected from behind the venetians, accompanied by the sound of a vehicle pulling into the driveway.

"Ah, good. That'll be Lokki," Madden announced, a trace of relief telling in his voice. "I hope you don't mind, Morris. He has someone with him."

"Like who?" Morris asked, somewhat peeved.

"My ex. Spider, would you be so kind as to get the door?"

Spider rose and crossed the room in compliance, opening the door just as Lokki arrived at the doorstep, with one large hand firmly placed around the arm of the woman he escorted.

She was around five feet ten inches in height, shapely and dressed in tight-fitting, white jeans and a floral blouse tied at the waist. Her cherry coloured hair elegantly cut to shoulder length, brown eyes and pale features gave her a refined appearance, enhanced by the items of fine, gold jewellery that she wore about her neck, wrists and on her fingers. Obviously high quality stuff and very expensive.

"You fucking bastard!" she shouted at Madden as Lokki guided her through the doorway. "Who the hell do you think you are?"

"Hello, my sweet," Madden replied serenely. "Taking a little impromptu holiday, were we?"

"I was going to Darwin to visit my sick uncle Charlie, if it's any of your business!"

"Lucky him."

Madden noticed the small traveling bag Lokki held in his other hand. He indicated for Lokki to throw it over, caught it, zipped it open and began searching inside.

"Hey. My personal belongings!" she protested.

"Shut it," he snapped, and continued to search. "Lads, allow me to introduce Gloria. Gloria, two of my business associates, Morris and Spider."

Gloria glared at both of them.

"Ah," said Madden, making a discovery, and digging deeper he came out with an airline ticket. "How long has poor uncle Charlie been unwell?"

"About a month," Gloria said.

"Don't remember you mentioning it?"

He opened the ticket to find the purchase date. "You bought this ticket last week, dear. It must have slipped your mind to tell me about it."

Gloria was silent for a moment. "I didn't want to worry you. I'd have been back in a day or two."

"Yes, of course. Very thoughtful. Why don't you come over and sit down? You've probably had a long day." Madden indicated the cane chair in the opposite corner.

Gloria eyed the position suspiciously before regarding the looming presence of Lokki beside her. "You made me miss my plane," she complained, moving to seat herself.

"That's a shame, baby, but it couldn't be helped," Madden responded, feigning sympathy. "For now, why don't we just sit down and have a friendly little chat?"

Lokki moved to stand against the wall, midway between the front door and the door leading to the central passage. Morris and Spider seated themselves on the couch, looking uncomfortable with the unexpected turn of events, but not knowing what to do about it.

"What's ailing your uncle?" Madden asked. "Hansen's disease," Gloria answered soberly. "Hansen's disease? Never heard of it. What's that?"

Gloria's eyes flickered with thought. "Slow disintegration of the spinal cord. He needs constant care and I thought I could lend a hand for just a little while. He is family, after all."

"Morris, you're pretty cluey. You know about Hansen's disease?" "Never heard of it," he lied.

"Eddie," she said plaintively. "I wouldn't lie about such a thing.

YIouwokunlodwn't. He needs constant care and the family needs all the help they can get. It's my duty to do what I can. You must see that."

"Oh, you mean like loyalty, that sort of thing? Yes, very important." "Then you do understand," Gloria simpered. "I knew you would.

You really can be a sweetie sometimes, can't you."

Madden made no reply, but studied her closely. Her eyes remained wide and unwavering in returning his gaze, her fingers busy with the ends of her tied blouse while a look of caution grew in her face.

"Eddie, why do you look at me so?"

Madden breathed in deeply, exhaled slowly. "Morris. Might we prevail on your hospitality? It's a hot night. Some refreshment, perhaps?"

"Beer?" Morris offered.

"Beer would be perfect," Gloria put in.

"Yes, a beer would be just fine," Madden agreed, and Morris rose to fetch them from the kitchen.

With Morris's absence, Spider was given an unimpeded view of Gloria. He stared lasciviously for a long time, until she shot him a piercing look which would have reddened his face, had it not been reddened already by the sun.

Morris returned, his arms laden with beers. "Here," he said to Lokki who appeared to be supporting the wall. "Hard work, standin'," he said good-naturedly, and Lokki accepted a bottle with a curt nod.

The rest of the bottles he distributed among the others, and tearing the top off his own he reseated himself beside Spider.

"Ah, yes," Madden intoned pleasurably, having taken a sip. "This is more like it. I haven't sat with friends this way for some time."

"Very jolly," Morris observed.

After a short silence Madden said, "You'll never guess who I ran into the other day, Morris. Remember Stephen Veech?"

"Stephen Veech," Morris puzzled. "I know the. . . Yes, little Stephen Veech, from high school?"

"Right. He's a lawyer now. I've hired him to draw up a business contract for me. I'm buying half-ownership of the Foreshore Restaurant. You lads will have to come down and sample the cuisine sometime. On the house, naturally. Seafood is the speciality."

"The Foreshore, eh? A good earner, for sure."

Madden giggled. "Very droll. Yes, it's always been an ambition of mine to own a restaurant. And I mean full-ownership, which won't be far down the track."

"Wasn't it Stephen's brother, Rudy, you nearly drowned when you threw him from the jetty?" Morris asked in diversion.

Madden chuckled. "That was a long time ago. We sure used to have a lot of fun back then, didn't we?"

"I suppose we did," he answered reflectively. "Or at least we thought we were having fun. We did some damn silly things."

"My brother and you were pretty tight in those days, I remember. Whenever Colin came home after a sortie with you, it always took him a couple of days to recover. And you wouldn't believe it, the old lady used to think it was you leading *him* astray. She never would see what a hell-raiser number two son was."

"Colin was alright," Morris said, remembering. "Never a dull moment." "I never knew you had a brother," Gloria joined in. "You never said."

"Had. Died twenty two years ago," Madden replied sternly.

"Oh, I'm sorry. I've got a sister, two years younger. I know I'd miss her terribly if something happened to her. How did he die?"

"Drug overdose," Spider chipped in.

Madden looked surprised, then turned angrily to Morris. "You also tell him it was me who gave him the dope!"

Spider answered before Morris could reply. "He only told me how him and your brother were good mates, and that he died from an overdose. Nothin' about that."

Madden was silent.

"I'm sure it wasn't your fault," Gloria consoled unconvincingly.

"Of course it wasn't my fault! What are you trying to say, that I killed my own brother?"

"No. I just thought-"

"He did it to himself. It was good stuff. I told him it was good stuff, and it was. I wouldn't sell my brother shit, would I? The damn fool was just too pig-headed to take heed. Thought he was superhuman."

In the silence that followed, Madden sipped his beer and quickly regained his composure. "Anyway, that was a long time ago," he muttered.

"I had a brother, too," Spider said.

"Who gives a damn?" Madden replied dismissively. "But I did. My twin brother, Taran."

"Was he an idiot, too?" Madden snapped irritably.

Morris rolled his eyes to the ceiling in vexation, wrestling with the simultaneous desire to see the evening out peacefully and Madden on his way, and the urge to read him the Riot Act.

"I ain't an idiot," Spider replied sullenly. "Neither was my brother."

Madden failed to acknowledge the remark, but after a while he gave a thoughtful snort.

"Remember when we first met, Gloria?"

Gloria's expression indicated discomfort. "You mean at Gordon Stanbridge's villa," she said with some emphasis.

Madden fixed her in his dispassionate gaze. "I mean at Regina's Emerald Palace. Your memory is not usually so poor. Regina's Emerald Palace, Spider," he said turning from Gloria, "is the name of a very high class bordello."

"Eddie, I don't think your friends would be interested," Gloria tried to interrupt.

"You know what a bordello is, Spider?" Spider shrugged. "A hotel or something?"

"Not a bad guess, but no. A bordello is a fancy name for a brothel. You must know what that is."

Spider's eyes showed that he knew what a brothel was. He turned to inspect Gloria with renewed fascination. "You mean...?"

"That's right," Madden replied.

"Why are you doing this?" Gloria demanded.

"I thought Spider might be interested to know how we met.

Every couple have a story. I guess I'm just a sentimental bloke." "You're going too far," she protested, rising from her chair.

"Sit down." His voice came low and even, but carried venom enough to convince Gloria to obey.

"She's a looker though, ain't she, Spider? You ever have a woman as good-looking as that on your arm?"

Spider squirmed uncomfortably, unable to reply.

"No, I don't suppose you have. It does a man proud to walk into a room with something like that. A real head-turner, and she's as smart as a whip. Conversation-wise, she can hold her own in any company. University education in science and economics. How do you like that? And with any number of career paths to choose from, what does she do?

"But she does have a natural talent for what she does, and that's a fact. My first night with Gloria cost a thousand smackers, and I was glad enough to pay." To Gloria, he said, "And then there are the fringe benefits, aren't there."

"I don't know what you mean," she said anxiously.

"Sure you do. But let's have a demonstration of how intelligent you are, shall we?" He turned to Morris and Spider. "You don't just have to take my word for it. Ask her a question. You go first, Spider. Anything. Anything at all."

Spider's face became a picture of concentration, and continued to remain that way.

"It's going to be a tough one," Madden scoffed. "Wouldn't surprise me if he stumped you right off, Gloria. Come on, Spider, we don't have all night."

"I can't think of one," he said, his face contorting to illustrate the effort he was making.

"Anything," Madden repeated. "Something you might have wondered about but were too dull to find out, or something you already know, if that's possible."

"I've got one," Spider announced proudly. "Okay. How far is a light-year?"

"Hey," Madden responded with surprise. "That is a tough one. How did you think of that?"

"I dunno. Just, when they say it on TV, you never know how far it is." "An inquiring mind," Madden noted sarcastically. "How did the lad slip through the education system?"

"My folks never made us go to school," Spider volunteered. "No shit? ... Okay, Gloria. How far is it, a light-year?"

Resignation was evident in her demeanour. "Approximately nine point five million million kilometres," she answered matter-of- factly.

Madden looked delighted. "See!" he beamed. "Now you, Morris." "Is this necessary?" he grumbled.

"Yes. Come on, it's fun. Stump the incredible Gloria and win a prize. Say, now there's an idea. I'll wager you can't out-clever her. You must know the answer and nothing too esoteric, I know you, Morris."

The idea appealed to Morris. The memory of money lost to McLeary still nettled, but this was an opportunity to take money from Madden! "Alright, you're on. Ten bucks?"

"Ten bucks," Madden agreed.

Morris leaned back and looked up to the ceiling for a moment. "Right," he said, leaning forward. "What is Newton's third law?"

Gloria smiled thinly. "For every action there is an equal and opposite reaction."

"Not so much a law as an axiom," Morris replied with some gravity. He dug awkwardly into his pocket and pulled out a ten-dollar note, rose and took it over to Madden. "You *did* say she studied science," he muttered, forcing a smile.

"Thank-you, Morris. Yes, I did warn you, but let's see if I can halt her winning run."

Instinct, or perhaps something less intangible, put Gloria on guard. "Let's not do this any more, Eddie. It's a bit tedious, don't you think? We don't want to bore your friends."

"Don't be a spoil-sport, dear. Everyone has to have a turn." Tangible or intangible, Gloria sensed a trap. Her eyes darted nervously from person to person, exit point to exit point.

"Oh, very well. If you must. But I have to go to the bathroom first, if you'll all excuse me for one minute."

"Stay where you are," Madden enunciated precisely.

"But-"

"I said to stay where you are. This won't take long, for a clever girl like you." When she failed to oppose, he said, "This time, why don't you have a bet on yourself?"

"I don't like to. I don't pretend to be so knowledgeable."

"But it was my impression you like to take risks?" To this Gloria remained nervously silent.

Madden was meditative for a while, then, raising a pointed finger, he said, "I'll tell you what. You come up with the right answer and I'll buy you that little sports car you liked so much. On the other hand, come up with the wrong answer and I won't. Does that sound fair?"

Gloria still looked nervous. "Come on, Eddie. What's the catch?"

Madden chuckled. "Trust me, there's no catch. But I am pretty sure you won't come up with the answer, if you want to call that a catch."

Gloria thought on it before giving the only reply she knew she could give. "Alright."

Madden smiled amiably. "A medical question, I think. By what other name is leprosy known?"

"Leprosy?" She made a face, either in reaction to the word or in being unable to come up with an immediate answer. Her concentration deepened. "Yes, I should know this."

Madden turned his attention to the couch where Spider scratched at the damp label on his beer bottle. Morris was far from preoccupied. He was taking as close note of Gloria's every action as he was. Morris was well aware, he knew.

He turned back to Gloria. She sipped her beer, deep in thought. "Ten seconds more," Madden informed her, raising his arm to view his wrist-watch. "I'm afraid your little blue car is looking doubtful."

Gloria's eyes sprang wide as her face betrayed sudden realisation. In an attempt to disguise this, she lowered her head and raised a hand to the side of her face, feigning greater focus. But now, she knew, she had far more urgent need for thought - clear and very rapid thought.

Madden counted down. "...three, two, one. Time's up. Ooh, too bad, you would have looked cute behind the wheel."

Gloria's face was pale. She tried to affect disappointment as best she could, but she looked more alarmed than anything else. With a good deal of pleasure Madden pushed home the advantage. "Your poor uncle Charlie, if he exists, and if he has Hansen's disease, is suffering from a condition known in layman's terms as... Morris? And I know you know as well as I. Your chivalry did not go unnoticed, earlier."

"Leprosy," Morris obliged.

"Your alleged uncle has leprosy? Madden asked threateningly.

Aware that silence could only be interpreted as guilt, she embarked on an explanation.

"I didn't like to say leprosy. I know it's terrible but, well, even today there is some lingering stigma. I didn't mean to be deceitful. Really, Eddie, I didn't."

"So just now you pretended not to know the answer, despite my generous offer?"

"I knew you suspected I had lied about visiting my uncle, so then I was afraid to admit the deception over his condition. It's foolish, I know, but I just couldn't let it be known there was a leper in the family. I'm really ashamed of myself," she offered plaintively.

The reply seemed to stall Madden for the moment, and he regarded her with something resembling astonishment.

"I offered you a sports car, which you sacrificed because of some perceived family skeleton? *That's* the flaw, although I've never before heard such an absurdly plausible story. If I didn't know you as well as I do, I might be inclined to give you the benefit of the doubt. But I do know you, don't I petal. You are, if not a gifted liar, at least a prolific one. Quantity outweighs quality, I'm afraid."

"I wish you wouldn't do this," Gloria responded. "I don't understand what's going on. Am I supposed to have done something terribly wrong? I was going to Darwin for a couple of days, that's all."

Madden chuckled mirthlessly. "Is that what you think this is about?" "Isn't it?" she rejoined, taken aback. "Why must you play these games?

And why, if you must, do you do it in front of people who are total strangers to me?"

Madden paused, not in considering a reply but merely to regard the defiant Gloria.

"Your brazenness, in almost any other circumstance, I would likely deem admirable. But I'm growing tired of it, and, to be candid, I find I'm not enjoying this as much as I had expected. "You are a conniving, lying, thieving whore, and I advise you to cease this charade now. You know very well what this is about, and I expect you to be woman enough to admit that you have lost this one. You will if you're smart. It'll be to your definite advantage, I promise you."

In unison, Morris and Spider swigged beer, waiting expectantly for Gloria's response.

Her face had been unreadable as she met Madden's words with measured dispassion. Now deliberation totally occupied her faculties, her eyes flickering in tandem, reflecting, perhaps, the swift sorting of facts required to accurately weigh possibilities against outcomes. Or was it fear in her eyes - fear that anything she might say would trigger Madden to violence, which, she knew, could erupt without warning?

"Eddie, please, consider the possibility that you might be mistaken. If you would just explain to me what this is about, I'm sure I could help throw some light on it."

"I gave you a chance," Madden replied icily. "And still you cling to your lies."

He launched himself out of his chair and crossed the room before she could do more than raise her hands in feeble defence. Grabbing the hair at the back of her head, he heaved her up and headed for the kitchen, dragging her screaming and wailing behind him. Morris and Spider made a move to follow, but were dissuaded from this by Lokki barring the way. Madden dragged her up to the table, pulled back the flap of rug and forced Gloria's face to within an inch of Owen's. Above her cries and sobs Madden bellowed, "See that! Is that explanation enough!"

Gloria crumpled, and Madden let her fall at his feet. He drew his gun from the underarm holster and swung his boot viciously, sending her sprawling backwards across the linoleum. As she looked up, shocked and startled, in a slow, deliberate manner he released the safety and aimed the thirty-eight at her face.

"Is there anything you'd like to tell me?" he growled, "or do you prefer to join your little playmate?"

"Alright, alright," Gloria gasped. "I took your damned money. But it was his idea!" She pointed to Owen's prostrate form.

Just then, Lokki stepped through the doorway, hands on head, in front of Morris who held a revolver on him, and Spider behind him.

"Got a slight problem, boss," Lokki said.

Madden was undeterred. "Come on in," he encouraged. "The show's just getting started."

Morris halted Lokki two steps inside the kitchen. "I don't think I agree with what's happening here," he said.

"Just hold it with that, will you Morris? Gloria has got something she wants to say, haven't you dear heart. Go on, tell everyone what you just told me."

Gloria quieted her snivelling just long enough to repeat, "It was Miles' idea."

"He told you what to look for and you did the thieving?" Madden prompted.

"Yes."

Morris chipped in. "Then you ripped off Miles and tried to flee?" "No. I was scared. Miles still had the bonds and he wasn't going to share. I figured that out. I was going to stay with a guy I met while I was on the game."

"So where's my fifty thousand now?" Madden demanded.

"I don't know, but fuck your filthy lucre and fuck you too. You know, you-really are a scum-bag, Eddie."

Madden fired three times, with measured delay between each. Lokki turned with the first shot and slammed Morris's arm, sending the gun pitching towards the ceiling as the two men wrestled each other to the floor. Spider dove forward, catching the gun in his right hand centimetres from the floor as Madden turned to monitor the action.

In the time it took him to sum up the situation, Spider had trained the gun on him, his own gun still pointing towards Gloria's bloody and lifeless body.

"Don't make me laugh," Madden snorted. "As if a cretin like you would have the balls."

Spider's countenance darkened considerably. "That was a pretty dumb thing to say," he replied with unbridled loathing.

Realization of his mistake struck as fear crystallised in Madden's eyes, and Spider shot him in the centre of the chest.

Morris and Lokki ceased their struggling with this fourth shot, and both looked over to see Madden dead on the floor. Morris, who had Lokki on top of him, holding two throttling hands at bay, looked up to his aggressor and said, "I think you could be out of a job, mate."

Lokki seemed to accept this as the truth, and rose, dragging Morris to his feet with him. "The missus ain't going to like this. Jobs are scarce." "I'd leave this one off your c.v.," Morris advised, and went to assist Spider, who at that momentwas looking a little weak kneed . "You still in one piece?"

Spider didn't answer, only handed Morris the gun.

"You look okay. Hey, buddy, them fireworks you hid. You still got them?"

"In my room," he answered.

"Thank Christ. Quick, go set them off in the yard before someone calls the fuckin' cops."

"Okay," he said, instantly setting off towards the hallway. Lokki stood up after having checked Madden for vital signs. "Dead?" Morris inquired.

". . .as a dodo. Bastard owes me wages, too."

Morris looked at him sideways. "How much is that then?"

"Dunno for sure," he said, scratching his head. "Around twenty five or thirty hours at thirty five an hour ..."

While Lokki worked on the problem, Morris rolled Madden over and slipped his wallet from his rear pocket. He flipped it open and pulled out the wad of high denomination notes. "Here," he said, handing Lokki half the money. "There's about two grand there. Don't blow it at the first fast food joint you come across. And your old lady doesn't have to know you're out of a job, does she?"

Lokki gave it a moment's thought and broke into a smile... "Yeah!" "Now you had better get out of here, man, while the goin's good, like they say."

"You need a hand or something?" Lokki offered.

"Yeah. Tell me what the hell I'm going to do about all this!"

Lokki looked around, then turned back to Morris, a blank look on his face. "You're just cluttering up the place more," Morris remarked. "You'd better beat it."

Lokki took Morris's advice and departed without further discussion. Alone amid the carnage, Morris uttered quietly, "If the landlord saw this he'd flip out." And from the back yard came the rapid-fire explosions of Spiders firecrackers.

DOIN' THE BOLT

ONE HOUR BEFORE dawn, in Owen's upstairs room, Morris sat wearily surveying the surroundings. Owen lay stretched out on the couch where Morris had placed him, after unwrapping him and wiping off most of the plum jam, beetroot juice and axle grease which had served well enough in convincing Madden of his violent demise.

In front of the couch, his back leaning against it, sat Spider, before him the bodies of Gloria and Madden wrapped in Polythene sheet which Morris had salvaged from a dumpster at the rear of a nearby supermarket. The remainder of the night had been spent cleaning the house at Clovelly Avenue, starting with mop and bucket and finishing with surface cleaner, in attempt to remove any trace that anybody apart from Morris and Spider had ever set foot inside the premises. When everything was as clean of incriminating evidence as it was possible to achieve, they had loaded their belongings into the van which Spider then drove to the parking bay at the top of the hill near Owen's house. There he had waited until Morris pulled Madden's car into Owen's driveway, with Gloria, Madden and Owen piled up on the back seat.

The cocktail of antidepressants, red wine and, after he had fallen unconscious, heroin, had produced in Owen the condition Morris had hoped for: his shallow breathing beneath the rolled rug going unnoticed. Now his breathing had returned to normal, with an occasional snort and half-turn in searching for a more comfortable position.

Morris looked across to Spider, who, like himself, seemed completely satisfied just to sit and rest. The day had taken its toll, and at this early hour mind and body were sluggish for want of sleep.

"What are you thinking about?" Morris asked.

"I was thinkin' about how me and my brother used to talk. Mum used to send us up to bed early sometimes, before her friends came round. We used to talk for hours before we got tired and fell asleep."

With some effort Morris focussed his eyes on his friend, trying to imagine him as a small boy of eight or nine years old. The knack eluded him until he stopped trying and simply viewed Spider as he was, sitting at the foot of the couch with his knees hugged up against his chest.

"What did you used to talk about?"

"Mostly about stuff we'd do when we grew up."

"Yeah," Morris replied with a soft chuckle. "I'd forgotten about that. Every kid can never wait to grow up. Grown-ups could do anything in the world they wanted to do. And kids. . . well, they were just kids."

"What did you want to do when you grew up?" Spider asked. "Me? Oh, I don't know. I think maybe I wanted to be an explorer." "An explorer," Spider repeated, much taken with the idea. "That's a good one. Why'd you choose that?"

"I suppose it came from reading so many of those boys' magazines. *Great Adventures, Pathfinder, The Wild* and all the others of that ilk. I always imagined the world being an endless expanse, full of undiscovered wonders and just waiting for someone like me to come along to find them."

"You ever been exploring?" Spider asked.

Morris shrugged. "Some. I've made a point of seeing about all there is to see in this country. Or at least everything I wanted to see. I've never been *O.S.*, unless Tasmania counts. But I read somewhere, once, and I think I probably agree, that the greatest adventure of all is the human experience."

Spider thought on this for a while before replying. "What does that mean?"

"It could mean that you don't have to strive in search of some great adventure all your life, when life, itself, being human, is already *the* great adventure."

"Who said that? Someone rich?"

"Probably," Morris replied, too weary to take it further. "What about you? What did you want to do when you grew up?"

"Lots of things. A cowboy, mostly." "What, like Kit Carson or Roy Rogers?"

"No, a real cowboy! You know. Mustering, branding, boundary riding and all that."

"A stockman, you mean. Tough work. An old buddy of mine runs a cattle station up near the northern border. Took it on after his uncle left it him in his will. Doin' alright, too, last I heard. What about Taran? Did he want to be a cowboy as well?"

"He like animals. Said he wanted to work in the zoo and let them all free. Especially the elephants. He liked them best."

"Yeah, I like elephants, too," Morris confided.

Conversation ceased for the moment, each allowing the other to lapse into private contemplation. Beyond the room came the steady crash and roll of waves at the base of the cliff, and the strident calls of gulls as they sailed the up draught in the pallid light of false dawn. Nearby, a car engine was coaxed into life, and in the distance, the roar of a motorcycle accelerating away.

The silence within the room continued for a long time, until Spider raised his head which had been resting on his knees.

"I'm sorry, Morris. I've made a lot of trouble and I don't know how to make it right again. I think I should just give myself up. I'll wait 'til you get clear, and you know I won't drop you in it."

"No. I'll think of something," Morris said firmly.

"I don't want to get you in trouble," Spider persisted. "I killed someone. You did everything you could so people wouldn't get hurt and I blew it." Morris shook his head, resisting the argument. "There's no blame for you to shoulder. None at all. Shit, if I'd had the gun in my hand at the time, I'd have done the exact same thing. The bastard snuffed her right in front of us. He got what he deserved, and if you'd been wearing a uniform and a badge, you'd be getting slaps on the back and told what a great bloke you are."

Spider shrugged disconsolately. "I don't think that's why I killed him," he said quietly, and let his chin rest on his knees.

Morris thought for a moment. "If you ever have cause to explain to anybody, you had better tell them that that *was* the reason, okay?"

"Okay, but I want to tell you the truth. You're my friend and I want you to know. It was like killing my father, I just couldn't stop myself."

Morris could find no reply.

"My father used to beat on our mum. He used to beat on us, too, but he didn't drink. Mum was the one who drank. We were always scared when he came home, so we'd stay out as much as we could and only go home when we got hungry. But then he'd get angry 'cause of that and we'd still cop it.

"Then one time the neighbours called the police. Mum was all bloody and beat up and he went to gaol. We thought that was good, and it was, I reckon. Everything was good for a bit. But mum took to drinking again, real bad. Me and Taran hung out in parks or at the zoo or somewhere most of the time, but then he got killed and I didn't have anyone to be with.

"A few weeks after that, I got home and my father was there, only he was dead. Mum had poisoned him with something in a pot of stew. She went to gaol and I went to one of them homes, you know? But I kept running away until they got tired of dragging me back."

"Where's your mother now?" Morris asked.

"Don't know. I'm not bothered either. Probably dead with the drink by now."

Morris nodded. "Quite possibly. But, I'm sorry, I don't quite get the connection between your old man and Madden."

"That's okay. I don't really get it either, but that's what happened. It was like he'd come back from being dead. He hurt Gloria and he kept sayin' I was stupid, just like dad. When he shot her, I don't think I felt anything. I just got really calm. But it was *him* standing there, and this time I knew I was going to do something about it. All that bad stuff I could never stop, but this time. . . this time." He raised his hands, unable to crystallise the thought.

"I understand," Morris responded sympathetically. "But none of that stuff was ever your fault. You just got dealt a really crappy hand."

"I know that. I do know it, but that still doesn't help."

"No. I don't suppose it does, but you're not to go blaming yourself for what happened, then *or* now, you got that?"

"Okay," Spider said, a note of determination in his voice. "Thanks."

Morris waited awhile before asking tentatively, "They used to call your brother Spider, didn't they?"

With his chin on his knees and hugging his legs to his chest, Spider regarded Morris appraisingly. "You did work it out. I thought you might," he said, breaking into a smile. "No one else knows that."

"Then I'm honoured and privileged," Morris told him, reciprocating with a smile of his own. "So. . . ?" He invited.

"So what?"

"So... your name, man. You going to tell me, or what?" Spider's face showed some apprehension.

"It's cool. I don't have to know."

"My name's Stewart," Spider told him.

"No kidding? Stewart? Yeah, you do look like a Stewart. So what do I call you from now on?"

"I don't know. I don't think I'd answer to anything but Spider any more."

"It would take some getting used to after all this time," Morris agreed. "Maybe if we work on it, gradual."

"That's alright with me, but what are we going to do? We're in big trouble!"

"Yeah, right. I've been working on it, and you might have given me an idea."

Spider waited expectantly as Morris gathered his thoughts.

"That stuff about you wanting to be a cowboy reminded me about Jake, the guy who runs the cattle station up north. We could go there for a while, and it's not like we'll have to hide away or anything. We can work for our keep, probably get wages, too. There'll be plenty to do and I reckon we'd have a good time."

Spider's spirits lifted. "That would be great. Could we really do that?" "I don't see why not."

"But what about Miles?"

"What about Miles?" Morris returned.

"He lied to us and got Gloria killed. And he knows who we are. He can finger us, easy."

"I'm still thinking that one through," Morris said, becoming pensive.

After a moment he began to give voice to his line of thought.

"He can finger us, yes, but why would he want to? He would be connecting himself to some fairly grubby goings on. He's an accountant, remember. Any individual or any business valuing their reputation would disassociate themselves in a second. He'd know that for a cert. He would have to move on, start over again somewhere else. Does Miles strike you as being someone who could easily do that?"

Spider shook his head. "But would *he* see it like that?"

"I'd say so. Yes, he's as cunning as a shithouse rat. And come to think of it, what does he know about us? First names, appearances, what else?" Spider shrugged.

"That's it," Morris stated emphatically. And after the concoction of shit in his system, he'll be lucky if he remembers even that much. I do believe we stand a good chance."

"We don't have to kill him then?"

Morris looked aghast. "Is that what you thought?"

"Well, yeah, because of that, and because of the way he put the blame on her." He nodded towards the blanket. "He's a rat, like you said."

"We'll probably never know the whole truth, Spider. But however it went down, each blamed the other for something they both took part in. They must have known what they risked if they were caught out."

"But he gets off, scot-free!" Spider protested. "He deserves a kickin' at least, doesn't he?"

"Look, Spider, if he's guilty of something or innocent ... half to blame or wholly to blame ... who gives a rats? Is the onus on us to mete out his punishment? We really don't know the truth in any case. I say we grab the cash out of his safe and leave him holding the can. Is that retribution enough for you?"

"I forgot about the money," Spider said, his mood brightening again. "We'll buy us some cowboy clothes," Morris encouraged. "Got to look the part when we arrive. What do you say, compadre? Shall we saddle up and hit the old trail?"

Morris grinned with pleasure at his friend, the promise of a new life burning clear and bright in his eyes.

end

END OF BOOK ONE

BOOK 2

FOR YOUR PLEASURE

W OULD YOU PLEASE get off your backside and go do
the shopping I asked you to do two hours ago!"
Margaret demanded, standing at the opposite end of the
kitchen table with her hands on hips in a determined pose.

John looked up from the crossword puzzle which had
occupied him for the greater part of the afternoon, allowing the pencil to slip from his fingers.

"The baby is down for her nap, so you can get out
from under my feet while I tidy up. Maybe then I can relax
for a while myself."

"Yes, dear," he replied, pushing himself up from his
chair and moving lethargically to where the joint account
passbook sat atop the fridge, along with the collection of
unpaid bills.

"There's forty dollars left," Margaret said pointedly,
regarding her husband in a critical manner. "I don't suppose it's any good me telling you to stay out of the pub, is
it? As if you'd listen. Two beers, you hear me? Two. Here's
the shopping list." She handed him a piece of notepaper on
which the items were listed. "Get the groceries first. And
for goodness' sake, ask around the hotel if there's any work
going. If only I'd known what a shiftless lump you were
before I married you."

Avoiding his wife's accusing gaze he folded the list deliberately and carefully consigned it to his pocket before retreating from the kitchen.

"And you dare go near those machines!" she warned as he pulled the front door to behind him.

Although it was a bright August afternoon, his well-worn wind- cheater proved barely adequate against the unusual chill which had persisted since early morning. He moved languidly along the footpath, somewhat distracted and thoughtful, his whimsical disposition affected in the usual way by his surroundings: An impoverished neighbourhood where alike brick veneer houses crouched in quiet abjection against the hillside; varicoloured roof-tops blending into the distance in semblance of some dappled impressionistic townscape, every home representative of the others, merely a piece of the whole, dreary, picture-puzzle-like scene; yards overgrown and tangled, the odd few mown and neatly trimmed, yet every dwelling exhibiting some telling sign, the deterioration over recent years reflecting the general malaise which had gradually spread through the community, casting a cloud of uncertainty over all the valley.

His zigzag course along the hillside streets took him past the yard where a white Volks Wagon Beetle was parked amongst a patch of thistle; the house itself looking particularly the worse for wear. The little car sat on four flat tyres, age-yellowed paintwork pitted here and there with ulcerous eruptions where orange rust had broken through. Propped behind the windscreen a sun-warped cardboard sign rescinded the previous asking price of five hundred dollars: an angry red line drawn through it. "$150," read the alteration. "Mech Sound"—the dubious statement underlined.

The vehicle's continued presence here over the months had produced a growing uneasiness and discontentedness in John. Three or four times a week—whenever Margaret sent him into town on an errand—he would follow this route along the hillside; and always, there it sat almost forlornly, its steady deterioration and now its inevitable drop in price hinting at what unhappy circumstance might lie behind it all. Strangely analogous, too; he thought of the changing character of the town, its sad decline from days more prosperous, more sanguine—far less careworn than present fortunes permitted. Ever since the closure of the nearby automotive plant, and with it the local ancillary industries. He and hundreds alike had been forced onto the dole queues. Slim hope of finding other work without selling up and taking the family elsewhere. But then the house was worth only half what he had paid for it those few years ago. Who would buy it! Who would want to live in this stagnating backwater town?

Margaret. She had grown cheerless and inflexible during these lean years. He had watched with mounting disconsolation her gradual transformation from the carefree young woman he had married, to the harried, ill-tempered wife and mother she was today; and for this, he felt sure, she blamed him. Perhaps justifiably.

At the base of the hill just ahead lay the town's main street where the majority of local businesses congregated. It was also the main arterial road connecting settlements south with the city some fifty kilometres away, and therefore carried much traffic, hardly any of which pulled into town unless for petrol from the town's single service station, or perhaps beer from the drive-through at the Morgan Vale Hotel.

At the street corner stood John's bank, a large, grey stone building of Gothic design, singularly imposing among the other buildings of the town, if only by size.

He climbed the five steps leading up to the front entrance and passed between the six broad columns supporting a massive portico. At its corners, gargoyles crouched overlooking the main street; extraneous and strangely at odds with the colonial heritage of the little town, John considered, pushing firmly against the brass plate on the heavy, red cedar door. His eyes reacted slowly in adjusting to the dimness of the bank's plush interior. At the counter, a grey-suited businessman waited, watching attentively while a teller counted out neat bundles of high denomination bills: Several thousand, John estimated. Easily enough to rid he and Margaret of debts, with maybe enough left over to purchase a second-hand car. That would be nice, he thought wistfully.

A self-mocking smile curled the corners of his mouth. He couldn't even afford the gun it would take to perpetrate such a crime. That's if he were that way inclined, which he wasn't. He viewed violence in any form with abhorrence. And dishonesty, well, he could truthfully say he had never committed a dishonest act in his life; never contemplated such a thing. In fact, it was terribly unnerving to find himself even entertaining the idea, however innocently.

Behind the glass partition, the female teller counted out his and Margaret's last forty dollars and pushed it under the glass. He accepted it with some embarrassment, inexplicably feeling the need to explain to the woman that it wasn't his fault.

There looked to be a disapproving glint in her eye, the merest hint of a sneer, and every time he came here it was the same. You're still on Government charity, the look seemed to say, and still you can't make the money last. When are you going to get a job? "Thank-you," he said in a voice far too timid, and hurried away towards the exit.

He was aware of being more than usually low-spirited today. Out on the street the blue sky and sunshine served only to intensify his discontentment, the feeling that he had been cheated in life; that he, Margaret and baby Marie had a right to expect much more than the lowly existence they were forced to endure, simply for want of a pay-packet and an adequate nest-egg to keep them in their later years. And there was Marie's future to be considered; twelve years schooling and beyond: The fees, the schoolbooks, dental and medical expenses. Even the basics were beyond present means.

Perhaps if he went away for a while; a job at a mining camp, some far-flung and isolated location where conditions were tough but the wages high. He wondered how many other men might already be vying for these positions, and how many positions could there be? And going away for weeks at a time, leaving Margaret alone to fend for herself and the baby, wouldn't that damage their marriage even more, or would the extra income prove to be the solution to their problems? The latter, he suspected. He would have to give it further, serious thought.

With his hands pushed deep in his pockets he followed the footpath past the bakery, the newsagent, the hardware store and the service station, oblivious to all but the constant roar and the exhaust fumes emanating from the traffic as it streamed past him, all the while locked in personal debate, uncomfortably recognising that he may have hit on a possible solution which could not now be ignored. One that, if it were to be acted on, would require greater courage than he had displayed in years.

The supermarket was now clearly in sight, but he hesitated upon drawing level with the hotel entrance, regarding for a moment the beckoning WELCOME sign displayed above the doorway. He recalled Margaret's explicit instructions—"Two beers. Get the groceries first"—and he turned again towards the supermarket which seemed more distant now than at first. The thought of a cold beer and a chance to sit and think presented itself seductively in his mind. Yes, he determined, he had important matters to chew over. The shopping could wait while he gave full attention to more pressing concerns.

He chose the saloon bar where he knew it would be peaceful, the atmosphere conducive to quiet contemplation, and swinging open the door and stepping into the warm, cheerful ambiance of the room, he saw right away the merit of his decision.

Working behind the bar was a tall, attractive, middle-aged woman with blond hair piled up on top of her head and held there with clips. Her large breasts were emphasised by the low cut of her serving-wench costume, a re-creation of the Elizabethan period which Management insisted its female staff members conform to. As John entered, she looked up from the conversation she was engaged in with three men at the bar—her only customers—and moved to one side to await his arrival.

"What'll it be, love?" She asked cheerfully, offering a wide smile.

"A pint of the standard, please, Annie," he replied, unable to match her good humour.

He paid for his ale and carried it to a table near the centre of the room, seated himself and looked up to the television sets mounted on the wall above a frosted glass window. On one screen horse racing was in progress. The other displayed race results and the current betting odds. It was a pastime he cared little for.

He quenched his thirst with a mouthful of the cool amber fluid and set down the glass with a satisfied clunk, lit a cigarette and relaxed into his chair, blowing a plume of smoke into the air. Already he felt so much better.

Over his left shoulder glass panel doors provided a view of the *Game Room* where poker machines stood in their rows, each one attended by impassive-faced towns-folk: men and women sitting unblinkingly, feeding coins into the slots, anticipating at any moment to experience the thrill of *the big win*.

Perhaps —he thought on reflection, turning back to examine his beer—derision was not entirely warranted. Since the machines had been installed six months ago, which in itself had caused a minor sensation, those people who would not normally be caught dead in such an estab-lishment, had taken to making regular visits. The ladies quickly adopted it as an opportunity to don their finer apparel, those items of clothing which otherwise would remain closeted for lack of a suitable venue, and even the menfolk had taken up the trend. A visit to the *Game Room* had become something of an occasion, a communal event, almost, yet with none of the usual interaction one might expect among such a gathering.

The pokies were a solitary pursuit, John recognised. They required a measure of concentration. Indeed, it was only five days ago that he had chanced his own luck and walked away ten dollars better off. But that was the trick, he mused. You had to know when to quit. *Always quit while you're in front, and never chase after a loss.*

On the television screen, racehorses lined up behind the barrier ready to jump. He picked number ten, just for fun of it. *Big Poluka* — a name he found on the adjacent screen. Margaret. . .

Right now she would be busily cleaning the house as she did every day, whether it needed doing or not. Vacuuming the carpet, curtains and lounge suite, polishing the table, dusting the shelves and venetians, positioning the chairs, books and knick-knacks, just so, until everything met exactly with her requirements. It had become almost an obsession with her. Perhaps it was her way of coping with their dreary existence, the ever- recurring tedium that awaited them every morning upon waking. Each day a featureless expanse to be traversed, stretching endlessly outward, with always the same grey horizon.

What did she think about while she worked? It was impossible to tell; her face set grim and unreadable as she rubbed at a particularly stubborn spot or raked hard at the carpet with the vacuum nozzle, no hint of what thoughts or emotions might lie behind those dark brown eyes. Instinct warned it was best not to disturb her at these times. He was mindful not to intrude on her privacy but, too, he never dared ask for fear of what she may reveal — what sphere of contemplation provoked so pensive a visage. There was so little conversation between them of late. *Real* conversation, not merely rhetorical comment followed by a disinterested reply. Some days, hours would elapse without a word passing between them. Then an argument might erupt for no particular reason, hurling them both into painful invectives, only to pass as suddenly as it had come, leaving each feeling wounded and resentful, to fall once again to dumb circumspection until attention to some trivial household concern required communication. How had he allowed things to slip to so miserable a condition?

His attention returned to the television screen in time to watch Big Poluka race past the post, six lengths ahead of its nearest rival. The screen alongside showed the odds at forty to one, and his heart sank as he stared disbelievingly at the readout.

A rank outsider. If only he had backed it. If only he had put a dollar on it.

Boisterous laughter issued from the three men at the bar. One of the group had tossed a peanut into Annie's cleavage—a great source of amusement for him and his buddies as she searched her bra to remove it, affecting a pained expression, half amused but mostly annoyed.

The tall man in the business suit John recognised. His name was Simcox and he managed the car-yard next door to the pub. Well shod and probably doing it easy, John imagined, moodily taking another swallow from his pint glass.

Simcox separated from his companions and John averted his eyes as he passed close to his table on the way to the men's room, though not before noticing the expensive gold watch on his wrist. He had seen one like it before, in a jeweller's shop window, and he remembered how he had scoffed. Two thousand dollars was more then he could possibly put by in a year!

Reflexively, he brought the glass to his lips in effort to swallow his resentment.

After a minute the door of the men's room creaked open behind him and he turned to catch Simcox's eye. He was a tall well groomed man, barely thirty years of age, by John's estimation, which would make him twelve years his junior.

He was about to pass by the table when John uttered falteringly, "Mr Simcox?"

Simcox started a little, caught by surprise, then halted, composure recovered and searching John's features with quizzical interest. "Yes?"

"My name's John Edwards," John began nervously. "I live just up the hill aways." He hooked his thumb over his shoulder to indicate the direction. "I was wondering... ah, I'm looking for work. if there's anything I could do at your car-yard."

Simcox slid his hands into his trouser pockets. "What do you do, John?

Mechanic, sales perhaps? We might be able to work something out." John disengaged from the unwavering blue eyes looking down at him,

watched the formation of wet circles on the table-top as he idly rotated his glass.

"No," he replied, looking up. "I used to work in the building trade, but, as you probably know, that's all dried up now. Then on the production line at the automotive plant, until they closed and moved interstate. But I'm handy with cars —— always serviced and repaired my own."

Simcox nodded. "We can only use certified mechanics though, John. Even if it's only an oil change or a nut that needs tightening. It seems silly, I know, but the trade is very strict concerning workshop personnel, I'm afraid."

"Yeah, I figured," John replied glumly. "But how about detailing, wash and polish, sweeping out the workshop? It wouldn't have to be full-time, even just a couple of days a week would do." "Sorry," Simcox responded sympathetically. "I'd like to help. I've got a lad who does that sort of thing."

John nodded. "Oh well. I thought it was worth a try."

"Of course," Simcox agreed, shooting a look to the bar where his friends awaited his return. "Well, good luck," he withdrawing. "Sorry I couldn't help out."

"That's okay. No worries."

When Simcox had rejoined his drinking buddies, he drank down the last of his beer in one go.

For a moment there he had thought he stood a chance. He could have gone home to Margaret with the good news. How pleased she would have been; a little extra money to buy the things they had to do without. The telephone could have been reconnected. She could have phoned her mother on weekends like she used to. The difference it would have made.

He looked at his empty glass in contemplation, tried to push aside his unwanted and unexpectedly bitter resentment. There was still the shopping to be done, he reminded himself, then stood and walked to the bar. He would have his second beer now, go straight home from the supermarket. Today he would make his absence from home last as long as possible. He wished he didn't have to go home at all, and he realised he had never felt that way before.

Returning to his table with a fresh beer, he sat and looked up at the television screen as the race-caller announced Little Devil the winner in the fifth.

At this, one of Simcox's companions, a stocky fellow with curly red hair, whooped excitedly, waving his betting ticket before him.

"*Little Devil*. You *little ripper*," he cried. "That's two hundred smackers. Annie, drinks for my friends!"

And Annie set about mixing drinks while the three concerned themselves with a selection in the sixth race at Strathalbyn.

John was staring into his beer in sombre contemplation when, a moment later, the lucky winner called across the room to him.

"Hey, matey. You like Irish whiskey?"

"I guess so," he answered awkwardly. "Yeah."

"Good. Then have one on me. It's only money," he declared, breaking into uproarious laughter and turning back to his friends.

The man's cavalier attitude and good humour brought a smile to John's face. Wanting to share in the fun he accepted the offer, surprised and delighted to be included in the celebration.

Annie brought the drink to his table: Irish whiskey and dry ginger. A double, he discovered, upon tasting it. It tasted good. He took another sip and set it back down, reached for another cigarette. He was beginning to relax much more now and enjoy the simple freedom of a quiet drink at *the local*. . . For a short time at least, free from the pressures of everyday existence.

Behind him a young couple entered from the Game Room, laughing quietly at some shared confidence, folding their winnings and pushing it into their pockets.

"Shall we try again after a drink?" asked the young man.

"No, that's enough. Let's not blow it," she replied, patting the money inside her pocket.

"We can have a great weekend if we hang on to what we've got." "Alright," he conceded grudgingly. "But I think that pirate game was about to pay out big."

They went to the bar and purchased their drinks, then carried them to a table near to where John sat. The young woman glanced over, catching John's eye as she lowered herself into her chair.

"Hi. . . Have a bit of luck?" John enquired, smiling. She hesitated. "Some," she replied guardedly.

"Maybe you're lucky for one another?"

No reply was forthcoming, only flushing cheeks and a demure expression before turning to her boy-friend.

He and Margaret were once like that, he remembered. *Love*, most people would call it. 'Those two are in love,' they would say. But he would reserve that particular word for something less fleeting, something which, if luck were on their side, would come in time, after sharing not only the good times but as well weathering the adversities and misfortunes it was life's custom occasionally to deal out.

These kids were infatuated, but then that was enough too. He secretly wished them both happiness as he reached for his whiskey and drank until the glass was empty.

He thought back to almost two years ago, the night Margaret had given birth to baby Marie, and how he had very nearly failed to enter the delivery room. To not be present would have been to deprive himself of what could only be described as a revelation. Something deep and abiding had touched him through that experience. At the moment of birth, life and love had become one and inseparable. The pain Margaret had endured and accepted in order to bring new life into existence, and the profound joy experienced regardless of it — it was the quintessential moment of John's life. The instant of realisation, when at last he understood what the word *love* truly represented, and how utterly the word failed to convey the all-encompassing nature of the phenomenon. So much wonder, joy and tenderness had filled his heart, he hadn't known whether to laugh or to cry. Unashamedly, he had done both. A new baby girl! They were a family and he would make any sacrifice to provide for their welfare.

John's eyes re-focussed on present surroundings. He instantly recognised the destination to which his thoughts were leading and willed the remnant images from his mind.

Making himself miserable would only compound the problem and he wanted to be in a good frame of mind when he arrived home.

Yes, he thought determinedly, taking a large gulp of ale. What was needed was a positive outlook, a no-nonsense attitude with perhaps a bit of common luck. . . and wasn't it true that a man made his own luck? Yes — Absolutely.

These thoughts filled him with renewed vitality, giving rise to some of the old confidence which had so long lain dormant. The coals had been rekindled and fire took hold anew. Clearly now, he saw how easily it all could be turned around. Change would be wrought. He drank ardently from his pint-glass. There was hope again. . . Better than that. He had, during this peaceful interlude, glimpsed a powerful and self-evident truth, one which would guide him unwaveringly from this moment on. Ponderous wheels turned and delicate balances shifted. . .

Whatever the nature of those capricious currents which exert influence over a man's life, fortune's eye once again deigned to regard him beneath its beneficent gaze. The allotted portion of cosmic goodwill to which every man was heir from birth was once more made accessible to him. He knew it; he could feel it in the visceral tremblings as excitement mounted — as every thought began to crystallise perfectly and with total clarity within his mind.

Harsh strains of synthesised arpeggios met his ears upon entering the Game Room. Snatches of vaguely familiar melodies piped out from every quarter, filling the room with a continuously shifting cacophony.

He stood confidently just inside the doorway — buoyed by the certainty of his providential reprieve, secure in the knowledge of his fateful return to grace, the plush blue carpet yielding luxuriously underfoot as he surveyed the scene before him.

Beneath a sparkling orb suspended from the ceiling at the centre of the room, narrow aisles provided cramped access to the ranks of chattering componentry. Hotel staff, smartly dressed in navy and white uniforms circulated nimbly through the throng carrying drinks, emptying ashtrays, fetching change from the cashier's window and where necessary adjusting troublesome machines.

From the end of the row in front of him came the rattle of winnings spilling into a collection tray, the shiny dollar coins expelled in rapid machine-gun like succession. Ten, twenty, thirty, John estimated. Sixty, seventy, eighty, while those nearby looked on with a mixture of envy and delight showing in their faces.

At the cashier's window he exchanged ten dollars for coins in a cup, and had to squeeze sideways through the queue at the bar in order to begin the search for a vacant machine.

Ten dollars was a lot. If Margaret could see him, now, she would have a fit. But she couldn't and anyway, what need for concern? All would be well, he knew this as surely as he felt the blood surging through his veins.

Rounding a corner at the end of a row, he saw an old lady climbing down from her stool. He advanced purposefully but the woman looked up in detecting his approach, a furtive shine in her eyes as she leaned the stool forwards and propped it against the machine.

"Going to the ladies' room," she announced warily, retrieving her handbag from the ledge but standing her ground until John had sidled by, to try further along the row.

Near the far wall he noticed a man abandoning his machine. The stool remaining upright and vacant. As he came closer, he made out the bold caption in gold letters at its top.

TREASURE CHEST, it read. There was the stylised depiction of a pirate, a desert island and X marks the spot.

Anticipation surged as he took possession of the machine and seated himself. With a silent invocation sent up, he fed two coins into the slot, selected his bet and triggered the relays into life.

**PIRATE + PALM-TREE + PALM-TREE +
X MARKS THE SPOT + PARROT**

**TREASURE CHEST + ISLAND + PIRATE
+ JOLLY ROGER + C+ANNON**

**CANNON + PALM-TREE + ANCHOR +
COMPASS + X MARKS THE SPOT**

Cool Hand — the guys at the factory had dubbed him that.

The memory emerged unbidden. . . On his first day he had been put to work on the line installing electrical wiring inside the skeletal car bodies as they inched along the factory floor.

By the second week his work-mates were seen to occasionally look up and take note of his activity, glancing intermittently at the clock above the supervisor's door as John worked dexterously with bundles of multicoloured wires from front to rear of the shell.

"It was a Saturday morning — *beloved overtime* — and his fourth week on the job. John gathered up the long electrical loom from its packaging and bent to the task. Miguel's thumb pressed down to activate the stop- watch concealed in his overalls pocket, and one by one nearby co-workers put aside their tools and moved away from their work areas, the better to view his progress.

John's hands worked independently, making connections one and two at a time in a continuous, fluid movement which seemed effortless as he worked from the headlight cavities, through the ignition system, under the cramped confines beneath the dashboard and down along the interior channel to the rear of the vehicle, finally connecting brake, indicator, park and number-plate lights.

Only upon straightening himself from the hollow of the boot did he realise the interest he had generated. Twenty of his colleagues had encircled him, expressions of admiration plain to see.

Miguel peered hard at the dial of the stop-watch, being careful not to make a mistake, then raised it high in announcing:

"Twelve minutes and forty six seconds. Nine seconds under the record!"

Enthusiastic cheers had risen from all who had gathered to witness the event.

**PALM-TREE+ ANCHOR + PALM-
TREE + COMPASS + PIRATE**

**X MARKS THE SPOT + COMPASS + COMPASS
+TREASURE CHEST+ PALM TREE**

**JOLLY ROGER + ANCHOR + PALM-
TREE + CANNON + PARROT**

:WIN10

He had made a lot of friends there. Sometimes after work they would meet at Taffy's Bar and down a pint or two before going home. There were the occasional barbeques, too, taken turn about at each other's homes. And the family outings organised by the social club; sometimes a cricket match played in tranquil surroundings at a country town oval, a day trip to the beach or a sporting event, tickets and coach supplied at minimum cost. There had always been something to do, if only a beer and a game of pool or darts with the boys.

**ISLAND + ISLAND + ISLAND + JOLLY
ROGER + X MARKS THE SPOT**

X + X + JOLLY ROGER + JOLLY ROGER + PARROT

CANNON + PALM-TREE + CANNON
+ ANCHOR + ANCHOR

:WIN 25

"Would you like a drink, sir?"

John twisted around to find a pretty girl in a serving-wench costume beside him, a silver tray cocked against her hip.

"We have a special promotional offer today," she added before he could reply. "Thunder Ridge whiskey at half regular price."

John hesitated.

"Why don't you try one?" she urged, flashing a perfect set of pearly whites. "If you don't like it there's a thirty per cent refund."

He looked at his total saw that he was over ten dollars up.

"Okay. I'll have a double with dry ginger," he said, wondering at his extravagance even as the words passed his lips.

PARROT + PARROT + PARROT
+ CANNON + CANNON

:WIN 25

He lit a cigarette and looked about with detached interest while attempting to judge how others in the room might be faring. Some sat, staring dully ahead, pressing the play button with monotonous regularity, seemingly disinterested in the result. Others engaged themselves more vigorously, experimenting with the available choices of bet size and the number of lines played, selecting different combinations of these between every turn. Most looked to be totally absorbed in the pursuit; eyes wide to the motion of twirling symbols, bright and colourful before them, closely monitoring their positions as they randomly fell into precise ranks, regardless to entreaty, uncompromisingly demonstrating cold function in their meaningless assemblage.

After a considerable wait, the girl returned with his drink. He lifted it from the tray and took a tentative sip. It was a tad bitter, he decided, but thought better of saying so for fear of appearing ill- mannered.

"Fine," he told her, and paid the four dollars she asked for, then settled himself ready to resume the game.

JOLLY ROGER + JOLLY ROGER + CANNON + COMPAS + ANCHOR CANNON + ANCHOR + PARROT + TREASURE CHEST + ANCHOR TREASURE CHEST + X + PALM-TREE + PIRATE + CANNON

By the end of his first year at the factory he and Margaret had managed to put aside a modest sum of money; enough, they agreed, to allow them to take a short summer vacation. It would be their first since they had married and moved to Morgan Vale.

With an air of adventure they had risen an hour before sunrise and set off for the rugged beauty of the South Coast, the car packed with belongings and equipment in preparation for every foreseeable contingency, the rented caravan amply stocked with provisions.

It was hot that summer, the hottest recorded in twenty one-years, and the road, gun-barrel straight, shimmering in the heat haze for mile after wearisome mile, the featureless scrub stretching green- grey from roadside to the limit of sight.

When the engine overheated they waited, bonnet up while it cooled, the sun so ferocious that car and caravan both became impossible to occupy for fear of heat-stroke; and outside, the bush- flies, their number incalculable, gathered in wait to fall upon sweaty bodies, their relentless assault ensuring that either choice resulted in torment.

The price of petrol rose to a dollar and seven cents a litre. Roadhouses offered tasteless, scalding hot coffee and stale sandwiches at exorbitant prices. Before even half the journey was travelled, tempers became frayed; a dispute over the speed at which John drove — Margaret maintaining that he drove far too slowly — almost seeing the trip abandoned, with John peevishly threatening to turn the car around and retrace the one hundred and fifty miles home.

At six in the evening they arrived at Jupiter Bay, gloriously picturesque on the shores of the Southern Ocean. So too scores of like-minded holiday- makers ahead of them. Exhausted by the arduous journey and with the caravan park full to overcrowded, they were forced to search among a network of sandy tracks along the undulating coastline in hope of finding a suitable location.

The third time they became bogged was the worst, with Margaret caustically pointing out his stupidity in failing to book ahead, the sun, meanwhile, splendid to see, dipping majestically towards the turquoise ocean behind her while John, working bare-handed, feverishly scooped sand in an effort to extricate the stricken vehicle before darkness fell.

It was nine-thirty in the evening before the caravan was parked on solid ground: A cliff-top overlooking the sea, the sound of breakers rolling and thundering below; the myriad stars, bright and scintillating in the pellucid night sky above.

Margaret swung open the refrigerator door to retrieve the steak and vegetables she had planned for the evening meal, only to be repelled by a putrid odour. Her withering gaze as John struggled through the door, laden with items fetched from the back seat of the car, told him he had neglected to set the fridge running prior to departure. Margaret's last shred of fortitude deserted her in that moment, unleashing such scorn as to overwhelm the senses — a verbal assault unrivalled in John's memory. And so they had driven back into town, found a seafood restaurant which played country music too loud while they sat in strained silence at a cramped corner table, waiting for their order of fish and chips - the cheapest item on the menu at $12.50 each - and a carafe of cheap table wine.

Jupiter Bay was an isolated town, the nearest hospital being ninety miles away. They arrived there at two in the morning, and after an interminable wait he was informed that Margaret was suffering the effects of ptomaine poisoning: tainted seafood the obvious cause.

Her stomach was pumped, ameliorative solutions administered via intravenous drips attached to her arms which, in time, brought relief. John remained with her, uncomfortably propped in a chair at her bedside, listening to the haunting ululations of the rising wind beyond the hospital walls; and thirty-one hours passed before they emerged from the building, weak and weary, too tired to utter a word.

At first John assumed he had come to the wrong location, taken a wrong turn somewhere among the many diverging tracks which penetrated the scrub-covered terrain. But, no, *there* were the tell- tale tyre prints where he had reversed in with the van. But, where *was* the van?

Margaret peered intently at the empty site, her lips set grimly as her eyes discerned the parallel tracks, barely visible on the compacted earth, leading to the edge of the clifftop. John discovered those same signs. His heart chilled as realisation dawned: the parking brake he had forgotten to apply; the frightful wind storm which blew throughout the night.

**CANNON + PIRATE + TREASURE
CHEST + PALM-TREE + ANCHOR**

JOLLY ROGER + COMPAS + JOLLY ROGER + X + X

**CANNON + PIRATE + TREASURE
CHEST + PALM-TREE + ANCHOR**

The machine had already eaten up the meagre winnings it had yielded, and now it was about to claim his original stake. Intuition told him it was time to move on. This was not the one, yet the irresistible feeling of imminent good fortune still remained strong. He took a swallow of whiskey and pressed the collect button. Ten shiny coins spilled into the tray. With the whiskey in hand he was still ahead, but the trick now was to *feel out* the room, allowing intuition to guide him, because somewhere in this room, and sometime very soon, he knew he had an appointment with *Providence.*

Collecting his coins, he slid down from the stool and moved off to begin the search along the aisle to his right. Adopting an insouciant manner he wandered casually between the rows, poignantly aware of the tense involvement of those bent to the screens. Aware, also, of the dejected sighs as near misses disappointed, and the obvious absence of a single, strident arpeggio to stimulate the adrenals; a response which charged the blood and caused pulses to race with excitement. He sensed the ebb of enthusiasm about him while, for him, anticipation soared to new heights. No wins, it was a good omen; and it was as if luck precipitated to him now, drawn from every hopeful player in the room, like an electric current arcing the distance between them, entering his body, coursing to the core of his being where dwelt his very essence. This was it, he was sure. This was truly *it*.

Rounding the last machine of the row he recognised it immediately. How had he not noticed it before, unless — could it have been installed just now, while he was occupied with the other machine? And with all the other machines being taken, why, with the number of people scouring the aisles, were they blindly passing it by? It was certainly large enough.

Large and imposing, standing within an arched recess where a doorway had once been. Partly in shadow, there was something almost brooding in its appearance, in the way light, instead of reflecting from its surface, seemed captured, held to dance lambently over the lustreless metal it was made of — looking much like unpolished pewter tarnished by age — but of course that was extremely unlikely.

Elegantly ornate, its design fitted no accepted style that he knew of. Art deco, he considered, approaching, but no, not as he drew closer. The complexity of contours in relief; the strange angularity deceiving his eyes. Now, standing in front of it, there was clearly greater subtleties to be seen.

From a distance the style which put him in mind of art deco seemed to be the extent of its decoration, but there was infinitely more. Every centimetre of its surface was covered in tiny characters, hieroglyphs finely engraved, arcane symbols minutely etched within intricate reliefs which, through some trick of the light, appeared to flicker and move with a life of their own.

Overhead, positioned around the top of this extraordinary artefact, zodiacal signs represented in golden miniature lent an ethereal quality, and standing in contrast above these, figurines of deepest ebony peered out beyond the golden rim, fantastic creatures of myth and legend with eyes of shining emerald, of which only unicorn, minotaur and sphinx were familiar. The others, though unknown to him, he found a little disturbing, especially the humanoid form crouched on all fours, its face holding an expression of mischief and cunning, its eyes strangely penetrating. The stool that accompanied the artifact, too, was ornately crafted in the same ambiguous, dull-shimmering metal, with elaborately constructed curves sweeping downwards forming its legs. The armrests upswept and scrolled at the ends, the backrest upholstered in crimson plush.

A man in grey slacks, black shirt and tan-coloured sport jacket emerged from an aisle on his left, one hand clutching a coin cup as he searched for a vacant machine. His gaze swept over the unoccupied stool, prompting John to act quickly, and climbed up to take possession for fear that the opportunity be missed, although this seemed to go unnoticed by the man in the tan jacket.

He luxuriated in its comfort, so snug and accommodating it might be imagined to have been custom-made for him. It certainly outrivalled, by far, anything he had previously experienced. His hands tested the smooth scrolls at the ends of the armrests, and a laugh of pure pleasure escaped him, which he stifled quickly, looking around sheepishly to see if anybody had witnessed his bizarre behaviour.

A woman in a lime-green dress walked by without so much as a look in his direction.

Turning his attention back to the machine, it occurred to him that with all its fabulous adornment there was no captions or instructions, no registration of symbols or score value, not a single picture to illustrate the nature of the game. There were, however, the usual two rows of selection buttons, though unlabeled and not so usually fashioned of what looked to be mother-of-pearl, and what he assumed to be the play button, prominently positioned, multifaceted and gleaming like an exquisite jewel.

There was only one thing for it, he decided. He took a coin from his cup and thumbed it into the slot, surprised not to hear the customary rattle as it descended inside the works. There was no response. Neither a visual display nor the slightest sound emanated from the lifeless artefact, and expectation slowly turned to disappointment. Then, rapidly, one character at a time, words began to spill across the screen. Stylish, scarlet-red letters, spelling out:

>>>WELCOME TO THE FINEST RECRE-ATIONAL GAMING UNIT AVAILABLE: THE SERIES FIVE ALPHA MODEL.

OMNICORP IS PLEASED TO PROVIDE THIS FACILITY FOR YOUR PLEASURE AND AMUSEMENT AND TRUSTS YOU WILL DERIVE SATISFACTION AND REWARD FROM ITS UTILISATION.

>>>THE SERIES FIVE ALPHA OFFERS A SCHEDULE OF NINE CHALLENGING AND INNOVATIVE GAMES WHICH MAY BE SUBSTITUTED ONLY UPON COMPLETION: EACH GAME REQUIRING RESOLUTION TO ENABLE AGGREGATE POINT- SCORE TOTALISATION AND ELIGIBILITY FOR POSSIBLE BONUS . . . UP TO 10,000 MONETARY UNITS!!!

>>>NO BETTING LIMIT EXISTS UNLESS DEBIT EXCEEDS PRESCRIBED AMOUNT - AMOUNT TO BE NEGOTIATED IF NECESSARY.

>>>CREDIT MAY BE EXTENDED IF REQUIRED - CONDITIONS TO BE DETERMINED.

>>>FOR YOUR ADDED CONVENIENCE OPERATIONAL GUIDANCE WILL BE PROVIDED AS NEEDED THROUGHOUT YOUR INTERACTION WITH THIS FACILITY.

>>>FOR GAME SCHEDULE DEPRESS GREEN BUTTON ILLUMINATED AT RIGHT OF PANEL AND MAKE YOUR SELECTION VIA TOUCH-SENSITIVE SCREEN.

>>>OMNICORP ANTICIPATES YOUR FULL ENJOYMENT AND WISHES YOU LUCK.

*omnicorp accepts no liability for any loss incurred

He stared at the screen for a considerable time, until the peculiar red characters began to disappear as they had come, one at a time, to be replaced a moment later by the Omnicorp logo, a tri-star arrangement within a golden O, at the centre of which a silver double helix rotated slowly - a three-dimensional hologram which was fascinating to the eye. Beneath this appeared:

DEPRESS GREEN BUTTON
FOR GAME SELECTION

The caption winked on and off several times before remaining constant.

John regarded the screen approvingly, his expectation of imminent good fortune rising, like the flow of a tiny electric current deep in his vitals. He leaned forward to press the green button.

GAME SELECTION

1. FRUIT	x10	4. MAZE	x1	7. QUANDARY	x1
2. TAROT	x10	5. PORTALS	x5	8. ILLUSION	x1
3. WHEEL	x10	6. RECALL	x1	9. CHANCE	x1

After a cursory inspection, he touched
the screen at number one.

SELECTION 1: GAME 1. FRUIT x10

CHOOSE BET SIZE AND NUMBER OF LINES PER
GAME DEPRESS RED KEY TO INITIATE PLAY

Three lines of five assorted fruit appeared on the screen, poised to spin in the same tired old game he had played so many times before. He noticed that the two rows of buttons on the panel now displayed the usual markings denoting bet size and the number of lines to be played. Opting for three lines at ten cents a game, he pressed the red button and watched the little fruit pictures spin. Ten times he pushed the button and ten times he failed to win.

GAME 1.   SCORE: 0

TOO BAD BETTER LUCK NEXT TIME

GAME SELECTION

| 1. FRUIT | x0 | 4. MAZE | x1 | 7. QUANDARY | x1 |
| 2. TAROT | x10 | 5. PORTALS | x5 | 8. ILLUSION | x1 |

DEPOSIT ONE MONETARY
UNIT AND TRY AGAIN

He felt cheated. The machine's elaborate exterior and apparent sophistication were obviously only for effect. He considered this awhile, casting his eyes over the remaining choices before him, then shrugged. He would give it another try. Perhaps it was a tad too early to judge; besides, the damn thing owed him a dollar. He dropped another coin into the slot and raised a finger to the screen.

SELECTION 2: 3 WHEEL x10

A GAME OF FORTUNE ... WAGER AS MUCH OR AS LITTLE AS YOU WISH ON EVERY SPIN AND HAVE YOUR FORTUNE TOLD

A bright wheel appeared on the screen, decorated with stylised depictions of cosmological features including nebulae, galaxies, planets and dark, tunnelling whorls in representation of black holes. Over all, a fine, golden web was superimposed to striking effect, and around the edge of the wheel, enigmatic symbols were described on coloured segments which continuously shifted hue in an anticlockwise direction, all but a single white segment which remained unchanging.

"Hokum," John pronounced under his breath, and as he watched, the garish display was completed with the addition of a silver arrow, downward pointing over the wheel.

The whole picture then shrank, receding to occupy top-left of screen as centre screen was taken up with:

RED:	FORFEIT BET		BLUE:	PAY	x2
ORANGE:	FORFEIT BET		INDIGO:	PAY	x3
YELLOW:	FORFEIT 50%		VIOLET:	PAY	x4
GREEN:	EVEN		WHITE:	PAY	x100

ADDITIONAL BONUSES OR PENALTIES DERIVED THROUGH TRANSLATION

OF ACCUMULATED CORRINIC
PHENOGLYPH UPON COMPLETION

(for clarification press grey key)

John's curiosity was piqued. He pressed the grey button.

CORRINIC PHENOGLYPH ... ANCIENT SYSTEM OF ENCODED NUMEROLOGICAL AND GNOSTIC SYMBOLISM OF THE KYAEN. USED IN RELIGIOUS PRACTICES AND FOR THE PURPOSE OF DIVINATION, IT IS RECORDED THAT THE KYAEN PROPHESIED THEIR OWN CATACLYSMIC DEMISE.

THIS BY UNKNOWN KYAEN POET:

> Is notthe wheel a simple wonder, from
> circles are we born All that is. . . of cir-
> cles born, reflects the key symmetric A
> line complete so many times repeated
> In circles are wedrawn.
> copyright: Omnicorp Universal

TO RETURN TO GAME DEPRESS GREY KEY

This he did, and sat gazing with renewed interest at the wheel, peering closely at the strange symbols around its edge. *Corrinic phenoglyph? The Kyaen?* Codswallop, he concluded dismissively

DEPRESS RED KEY TO SPIN WHEEL

As if a lumbering thing, the wheel gained momentum slowly, until the whirling prismatic colours blended to white, bright and glowing, the alien symbols dancing in flickering, spasmodic fashion until, in slowing they began to roll, first one way, then the other, to blur and rotate as its speed began to rapidly diminish. Beneath the silver arrow a blue segment came to rest, the symbol on it resembling a crudely depicted giraffe more than anything else he could recognise.

SPIN 1: PAY x2   SCORE; 20   AGGREGATE: 20

"Ah-ha," he let out gleefully, and hurriedly set the wheel in motion again.

With growing excitement he applied himself to the game. One spin after another, he watched as his total steadily increased, though not by as much as he would have liked. With just two spins left to play, he sought to remedy the situation.

BET: 50   AGGREGATE: 130

He pressed the red button and watched helplessly on, eyes wide and unblinking as luck took control. There was a not altogether unpleasant gnawing sensation in his stomach as he tried to will the wheel to fulfill expectation.

The wheel slowed. His eyes widened further as a violet segment rose, arcing gradually towards the silver arrow, finally coming rest directly beneath it.

SPIN: 9 WIN x4   SCORE: 200   AGGREGATE: 330
(LAST SPIN)

He sat gloating over the numbers revealed on the screen. Three hundred and thirty. Three hundred and thirty dollars! He could scarcely believe it. But he had known he would be lucky today. He had felt it right from the start.

For the tenth and final time he spun the wheel, and watched, disappointed as it settled on green to leave his score unaltered.

PLEASE STAND BY A SHORT WHILE
FOR PHENOGLYPH TRANSLATION
AND POSSIBLE BONUS POINTS

John curled his lip disdainfully, although, in truth, he found he was more than just a little curious. He picked up his glass and drank the last of its contents, put it down and reached for a cigarette.

WOULD YOU LIKE ANOTHER DRINK? YES/NO
INDICATE VIA TOUCH-SENSITIVE SCREEN

"What?" he responded taken aback. "But how—?"

He stopped himself. He had observed others talking to themselves in front of these machines - *borderline nutcases* - and he wasn't one of them.

Perhaps the machine was somehow linked to a signalling device behind the bar? But then he wasn't particularly concerned with the technology of it right now. Another drink was a good idea though. He leaned forward to touch YES.

PHENOGLYPH TRANSLATION COMPLETED
HERE IS YOUR FORECAST

THE FUTURE IS ILL-DEFINED YET CLEARLY IN CRITICAL BALANCE. IMPORTANT DECISIONS MUST BE MADE AND ADHERED TO, ENSURING A FAVOURABLE OUTCOME. AVOID TAKING RISKS. COUNT WHAT IS DEAR TO YOU ABOVE ALL ELSE. THUS WILL YOUR TRIAL END AND HAPPINESS SURELY FOLLOW.

GAME 2: ZERO BONUS POINTS

TRANSLATION FEE: 5 AGGREGATE: 325

The forecast was a disappointment, typical of the vague mumbo jumbo to be found in any of the daily papers. But the fee, that was an outright insult. And where was the waitress to fetch his drink?

He swung around in hope to see her approaching. There was no sign of any waitress, and the aisles were jam-packed now. Punters bent earnestly to their screens, oblivious or indifferent to those who milled through the narrow aisle in hope of finding a vacancy.

Turning back to the machine, he glanced toward his empty glass. Only, it was no longer empty. He lifted it from the recess, ice- cubes rattling in the dark liquid, and brought it to his nose... Whiskey and dry ginger, there was no doubt. He took a tentative sip, *mm' d* and smacked his lips approvingly. No cheap imitation, this. This was the good stuff, he recognised immediately. And taking a good swallow, he set it back down feeling somewhat placated.

"Weird bloody machine," he muttered, again taking note of his total. It occurred to him that he might collect his winnings and go home,

but he had only just settled into the game; besides, he couldn't walk away yet. Who knew how much he might win?

The stories he had heard of people winning thousands — today he could become one of them. Wouldn't Margaret change her tune then!

GAME SELECTION

1. FRUIT	0	4. MAZE	xl	7. QUANDARY	x1
2. TAROT	xl0	5. PORTALS	x5	8. ILLUSION	xl
3. WHEEL	x330	6. RECALL	xl	9. CHANCE	xl

He leaned forward to make his next selection and was surprised by a tiny electric shock as his finger touched the screen. It sent a tingle up his spine and over his scalp, but he paid it little heed. Static electricity often accumulated in such places.

SELECTION 3: 6. RECALL xl

RECALL IS A SIMPLE GAME TO TEST YOUR MEMORY. MATCH ALL TEN PAIRS OF CARDS IN UNDER FIVE MINUTES AND WIN FIVE TIMES YOUR BET. UNDER TWO MINUTES WINS TEN TIMES YOUR BET AMOUNT.

DEPRESS RED KEY WHEN READY

John knew what to expect. It sounded just like the game he used to play as a child - a game called Concentration. And, sure enough, upon pressing the red button he was presented with four rows of five cards, face down, the Omnicorp logo displayed on their up side.

SIMPLY CHOOSE TWO CARDS VIA TOUCH-SENSITIVE SCREEN. MATCHING PAIRS WILL REMAIN FACE UP WHILE INCORRECT SELECTIONS WILL TURN DOWN AFTER A SHORT PERIOD.

A time-clock appeared at top-left of the screen.

REMEMBER TO REGISTER YOUR BET > GOOD LUCK

John smiled to himself. Twenty cards. Just ten pairs. As a boy he was pretty good at this game, and back then he had-played with a deck of fifty-two. Admittedly two minutes wasn't very long for the big win, but at worst he would win five-fold, he felt sure. Lifting his drink from the small recess, he took a good swallow, savouring the moment.

He had $325 credit. In one game he could turn it into $1,725 or even $3,250. But did he have the courage to go for it? Could he face the disappointment if he hedged, only to win the game easily.

He sipped his drink Yes, he had to go for it. It was too good an opportunity. Hell, he had gotten this far on two measly dollars. He would really only be two dollars down if he failed. But he wouldn't, he was about to clean up!

He took another sip of whiskey and screwed up his courage, set the bet at 325.

BEGIN WHEN READY

Nervously, he placed a finger on the screen to turn the first card, revealing a picture of a cute Dalmatian puppy. The second turned up a blue tricycle. The cards remained up-turned for two seconds longer, but just as they flipped back over again, some fleetingly perceived peculiarity upset his concentration.

The next pick produced a photographic portrait of a teenage girl, and the next, a second Dalmatian puppy. He faltered as recognition struck.

"It can't be," he whispered, his perplexed visage reflected back to him in the light of the screen.

He remembered the time-clock, noted its steady advance and recovered composure enough to force his hand to the screen. He picked two more at random, by fluke matching a pair of Holden cars.

Again surprise. *My car,* he gasped.

Clearly, it was his old Holden Premier — the number-plate leaving no doubt.

"Monty?" he emitted in disconcertion, recalling the puppy — his old friend and companion for so many years.

Again he turned a card, this time revealing a picture which at first made no impression on him — which, for a moment even defied identification. Then memory served, sending his mind reeling back through the years.

As a child he had been afraid of the dark, and he would often wake in the middle of the night to lie terrified of unseen monsters lurking in the darkness. His mother had bought him a night-light; a small, battery- powered lamp in the shape of a rabbit, moulded of opaque white glass and with red painted eyes, whiskers and ears. In the still depths of countless nights it had dispelled both fear and darkness, warded off fell creatures of imagination while a small boy's eyes remained fixed on this comforting object, every contour, every feature and imperfection etched in memory by the long hours of gazing, waiting for sleep's return and an end to the ordeal. And the teenage girl, he remembered, suddenly jabbing a finger at the screen to recall the portrait.

Gina. It was Gina, his first sweetheart. Again he jabbed at the screen: His old tricycle. . . and again: A small boy in a cowboy costume. *Him!* John Michael Edwards, age seven!

"It can't. . ." he attempted in a hoarse whisper — shock and disbelief strangling his voice. To the evidence his mind would not accept, his eyes remained fixed.

"It's not. . ." The words would not come. What his eyes beheld, *had* to be real: A slice of his undocumented past, maybe, but real nonetheless, and irrefutable.

So absorbed had John become by the images before him that he was, for the most part, unaware of the strange sensation which began in his extremities. A slight tingling, followed by warmth and mild numbness crept along his legs and arms into his torso, up along the spine to the top of his head where the warm pleasantness spread out over his scalp.

He turned another card. This one depicted a treehouse. How many hours had he spent in that rickety construction, alone in childish contemplation of the world and all the exciting things it contained, dreaming of the time when he would reach manhood and of all the wondrous possibilities that would comprise.

Another card: A grassy embankment. His favourite place where he used to lay watching the clouds float silently overhead. *Dirigibles, giant animals, cavalrymen on horseback charging headlong into battle. Rocketships, sailing-ships, adrift in blue summer skies.* Such peaceful moments preserved in memory. Days of innocence and tranquillity forever gone. Such a yearning rose up in his chest as to draw tears of pure joy.

Like a bubble bursting, the reverie exploded into thousands of tiny sparkles and faded to nothing. On the screen two words flashed, then held steady:

GAME OVER

Staring blankly ahead, his faculties were slow in deciphering. . .

SELECTION 3: 6. RECALL   SCORE: 0 TOO BAD

INSERT ONE MONETARY UNIT AND TRY AGAIN

1. FRUIT	x 0	4. MAZE	x1	7. QUANDARY	x1
2. TAROT	x 10	5. PORTALS	x5	6. ILLUSION	x1
3. WHEEL	x330	6. RECALL	x0	9. CHANCE	x1

AGGREGATE: 0

How had it done that? The question crystallised suddenly. My memories. My most private recollections. He ought to be angry, he considered. *Incensed!* But being confronted by so extraordinary a phenomenon, emotions deferred to an overriding sense of wonder, if not trepidation.

The screen remained impassive before him.

TOO BAD

INSERT ONE MONETARY UNIT AND TRY AGAIN

"You tricked me," he said, at last gaining a modicum of composure. "How did you do that?"

TOO BAD

INSERT ONE MONETARY UNIT AND TRY AGAIN

"You rotten, slimy, son of a–"

His enunciation was only slightly impeded, but sharp with resentment. "Too bad, eh? You cheated me out of more than three hundred bucks.

We'll just see about that. We'll just see."

And so saying, he dropped another coin into the slot — jabbed a finger at the screen.

SELECTION 4: 4. MAZE

THIS FACILITY IS NOW IN FULL
INTERFACE MODE

... STAND BY...

John waited. "Stand by for what, you thieving son of a–"

The Game Room vanished. For an interminable instant there was only vast emptiness — *ethereal, alien, and timeless* — so incomprehensible that the mind threatened to shut down in protest.

Had the moment been less fleeting panic might have set in, but transition had been mercifully swift; the unusual calmness which now wholly pervaded his being acted to cushion much of the impact.

Bizarrely, the fact that he was now standing struck him as being the biggest change, but that lasted only until delayed cognition kicked in, alerting him to the weirdness of his surroundings.

He stood beneath orange sky. Behind and to either side of him a dusty grey plain covered an enormous, featureless expanse, making distance impossible to judge. In front of him stood a wall of staggering magnitude.

Huge smaltlike stone blocks rising, immensely high, were fitted so precisely together that the seams, even close up, were difficult to detect and stretched in perfect alignment to the limit of.

When full awareness hit it came less as a shock than as a surprise, without the aura of lost reason or jolt of the fantastic, yet still with a *good measure* of surprise. The sheer, looming mass of the wall caused him a backwards step — an involuntary move which better allowed him a grasp of its size.

"What the bloody hell," he uttered in awe, then turned to survey the barren terrain and the vaulted orange expanse overhead.

At once recognising his predicament, and necessarily presuming he wasn't at this moment lying unconscious on the hotel floor suffering some kind of brain malfunction, he said aloud: "A bloke could die in this place if he wasn't careful. And there's no sun," he noted.

It wasn't hot here, wherever *here* was, and it was apparently devoid of life-sustaining requirements such as food, water and shelter. Things were not well.

In scrutinising his surroundings he turned full-circle, again to face the preposterous mountain of masonry. A darkening spot on its smooth surface caught his eye; small but enlarging steadily, growing in diameter until, at two metres or more, it reached ground-level, at which point it ceased. To his added bemusement, an aperture like a dilating iris opened within the circle, revealing beyond it a small courtyard, furnished with bench tables, chairs and striped umbrellas, all neatly positioned around a water fountain at the centre. Only the absence of gaudily clad tourists chatting pleasantly beside the cascade rendered the scene counterfeit.

"What in the blue blazes?" He leaned slightly forward, peering in through the opening. Then, appearing in mid-air between himself and the entrance came:

Game Commences

"Not on your Nelly," he said to no one in particular. "This isn't funny.

I don't want to play anymore, okay? Cut it out."

His voice rang out across the alien landscape and was quickly lost to distance, sounding small against the vast open space — puny beside the massive structure that towered over him.

"I'm not going in there."

The plain looked a fairly inhospitable place. Not a hamburger takeaway or a hotel in sight. The whole thing was, of course, quite impossible, he was forced to remind himself; although, the premise did seem somewhat irrelevant at this precise moment.

"Get me out of here!"

Needs must, was the aphorism which sprung unsummoned to mind. It didn't appear that whatever force was in control here was about to give way to entreaty.

"Please! I want to go home."

Nope. . . stuck here all right, and it didn't take an Einstein to work out what was required in order to get unstuck.

If he was being given a choice here, it wasn't much of one. There was *that*. He looked out at the flat, dusty expanse. Or there was *that*. He turned again toward the ominous-looking opening in the wall, and God only knew what else lay within.

"You damned, infernal, machine," he bellowed angrily, and shuffled resignedly towards the entrance.

He hesitated for a moment at the threshold, taking one last look over his shoulder to assure himself that there was no other option. And taking a fortifying breath, he stepped through.

The floor of the courtyard was paved in terrazzo, and the confining walls decorated with geometric patterns which he found strangely at odds with the general motif. As he moved closer to the centre an optical illusion became evident, effected by the divergence of lines within the decorative patterns, drawing the eye away. Corridors, difficult to hold focus on, but there, leading from the courtyard like so many spokes from the hub of a wheel, and stretching, no doubt, into the heart of the maze.

A pang of uncertainty caused him to glance back at the entrance. To his acute disappointment his eyes meet only with smooth, stone. His gaze followed the wall up to its high rim, where he discovered there was now a blue sky overhead; the inconsistency failing to surprise him. It seemed his capacity for surprise had about reached its limit.

The only sound to be heard was that of water splashing at the base of the fountain, echoing off of every stone surface. A pleasant enough sound, normally, but now tainted with a vaguely sinister quality as it resounded about the empty enclosure. Nevertheless, he found himself drawn to it.

He sat on a ledge beside the water, thoughtful as he watched the ripples distort the miserable looking reflected image of himself and the immediate surroundings. If he waited here for long enough, he began to reason, maybe the machine would abort and he wouldn't have to search for the way out. Anyway, how many exits did this monstrosity of a place have? There were no rules he knew of that said there ought only be one.

THERE ARE TWO EXITS

The answer came clear and steady on the surface of the water. He knew he shouldn't have been surprised. In fact he was *surprised* that he was surprised.

"You can read my thoughts?"

YES

"Then read this." *I don't like it here. Get me out!*

NOT YET

"Not yet?" Trying hard to sound surprised and affronted, though genuinely unwilling to accept the response. "What do you mean, not yet? You're a machine, aren't you? I'm the one supposed to be in command. Get me out of here."

GAME REQUIRES RESOLUTION TO DERIVE
AGGREGATE POINT-SCORE TOTALISATION
AND ELIGIBILITY FOR BONUS POINTS

"I choose to forfeit."

FORFEITURE UNACCEPTABLE
AT THIS JUNCTURE A LEVEL OF
PARTICIPATION IS REQUIRED

GAME HAS COMMENCED

"Damn you," he spat. "What the hell are you?"

THE SERIES FIVE ALPHA MODEL IS THE
FINEST RECREATIONAL GAMBLING
UNIT AVAILABLE ANYWHERE.

OMNICORP IS PLEASED TO PRESENT
THIS FACILITY FOR YOUR PLEASURE
AND AMUSEMENT AND TRUSTS YOU
WILL DERIVE BOTH SATISFACTION
AND REWARD BY ITS UTILISATION.

"Then you can bloody well facilitate my pleasure and amusement by getting me the hell out of here!"

UNABLE TO COMPLY AT THIS JUNCTURE
GREATER LEVEL OF PARTICIPATION
REQUIRED BEFORE ALTERNATIVE EXIT
OPTIONS BECOME AVAILABLE

"Oh yeah? And if I decide not to participate?" he responded peevishly.

Some seconds elapsed without response. A minute. Two minutes. "Okay, alright," he shouted, jumping to his feet. "I'll play your stupid game."

He swung about, taking a cursory account of the number of diverging corridors. "Alright?"

GAME IN PROGRESS

He growled deep in his throat and stalked off in a fume, meaning to choose any corridor at random, if all it took to get out of here was *"A level of participation."*

The moment John stormed into the corridor entrance he was plunged into darkness, and turning to make a hasty exit he was horrified to discover only more of the same, where ought to have been a sunlit courtyard framed by the stone arched entrance.

He froze in his tracks, the pitch darkness and utter silence augmenting his senses so that they reached out for any sign or clue, his nerves wound tight and straining.

"Damned machine," he whispered vehemently, the sound of his heartbeat pounding in his ears.

After he had stood this way for half a minute, his eyes began to glean what meagre light was available. Not so much pitch darkness now, as general murkiness; he started to inch his way forward, guiding himself by running a hand along the tunnel wall, the other outstretched to detect any obstacles which might lie ahead.

If the tunnel curved one way or the other, he was unable to judge; for all he could tell it ran dead straight ahead, step after step after step, each one counted as a means of determining his position should the need to backtrack arise, but more to occupy his mind in this utter darkness; in his mind's eye a child's bunny-rabbit lantern glowing, every detail remembered, *13, 14, 15 . . . . .*

Midway through his ninth year he had been sent to stay on his grandparents' farm. His mother had done her best to pass it off as a holiday, some kind of special treat, but a nine-year-old can detect the odour of deception a mile off, especially with his parents quarrelling being much fiercer of late, and going by the disturbing sounds to reach along the hallway to his bedroom some nights, he knew it had passed beyond mere angry words. Yet despite the obvious ploy of a holiday, and despite the deep resentment he suffered at his being shuffled out of the way as if he were no more than a complicating factor, his stay at the farm left him with the few pleasurable memories to come out of that turbulent period of his life.

In the habit of eating a bowl of sugary breakfast cereal alone in front of the television each morning, grandma's morning regime had come as something of a shook to the young John.

The unbending rule had been that he bathe before breakfast, and that he be at the table at the absurd hour of six o'clock. Only then was breakfast served up; such a meal as he had never seen at home, not even at dinner- time! Bacon, eggs, sausages, fried tomatoes and toast, all washed down with as much tea as he could drink. Even now, the profound impact of the first grandma's cooked breakfast had faded little with the passing of time. In fact, memory sought to preserve the experience as originally viewed, through eyes of astonishment, an exhibit in the museum of the mind where it remained forever undiminished to this day: the finest breakfast he had ever sat down to, *57, 58, 59, 60. . . . .*

And after breakfast there were the chores: the fences to mend, irrigation ditches needing attention less they clog, and fruit trees to prune, sheep to feed, cows to milk, mechanical repairs on the ancient machinery. Vegetables to gather for the larder; every daylight hour taken up in productive activity, *weekends included!*

Exhaustion saw him in bed by eight o'clock on most nights, where, ordinarily, he had rarely gone to bed before twelve, sometimes falling asleep on the couch in the front room, the television left on, marring any chance of a sound and restorative night's sleep. But at the farm, sleep soothed and reinvigorated.

Something important had been instilled during his time on the farm — something he had never forgotten. Until then he had never done a lick of work, not the real, physical kind. By the second week all soreness of body had subsided and there was a new-found pleasure in tautness of muscle and sinew, a genuine feeling of pride in a job done, and done well.

His grandpa enjoyed talking while they worked, and John liked to listen, mostly about the land and the weather and such, but never about the city or John's situation at home. Sometimes he talked of his experiences in the Great War, the Palestine campaign, the endurance and ever-faithfulness of a breed of horse called the Waler, acts of bravery and fallen comrades left to the sands of the Sahara. Stories that cultivated a boy's imagination with wonder and awe, related in an old man's wavering voice, deftly bridging the gap of years between them *102, 103, 104.* Was it his imagination or had the tunnel floor begun to slant ever so slightly downwards? He decided to stop counting his steps: The likelihood of a need arising to return to his starting point seemed appreciably less at this stage, and what returning would achieve in any case he wasn't too sure. The notion was really quite pointless. Yet he found himself counting, still. A portion of his mind was unwilling to forgo the simple exercise which continued to serve a comforting role. But, yes, he was quite sure, in the last five paces the floor had angled more steeply.

By the time he felt himself slipping it was already too late — the slope had been far greater than he had realised — confounded as he was by the darkness and some architectural chicanery, the sudden slipperiness of the stone floor had him sliding speedily down through the gloom, a howl of pure terror marking his passage.

Down and down he hurtled, blind and fearful, the sleeves of his windcheater snapping angrily through the rushing air—and accelerating with every passing moment.

A cry of surprise and anguish escaped him as he found himself held, careening against the wall as he followed a tightening curve; a downward spiral which turned his cry into a wail when, without warning, he was catapulted free a moment later to plunge into icy cold water.

He surfaced spluttering and gasping, flailing the water in a panicky attempt to reach the edge of the pool, and making it to the edge he hauled himself out, rolled onto his back and lay staring up at the high, curved ceiling. While his breathing steadied, his eyes began to distinguish the intricacy of colour and texture of the marblelike stone above.

He sat up. The cavern was roughly circular, the pool into which he had plunged so unceremoniously being at one end. There was no obvious light source, he noted, yet illumination was complete, without shadow or contrast.

He climbed to his feet, shaken and decidedly unhappy, watching disconsolately as water drained out of his sleeves. A look of alarm seized his features and his hand darted to his trouser pocket, his expression changing to one of disgust as he gingerly withdrew a sodden packet of cigarettes.

"You rotten mongrel," he intoned bitterly, and let them fall to the floor with a plop.

In consideration of what had just happened to him, loitering didn't seem a good idea. Even as he stood, staring down at the ruined cigarettes, he could feel the trembling after-effects of the frightful helter-skelter ride creeping upon him. Muttering a last, heartfelt expression of displeasure, he set off in an ungainly manner towards the other end of the cavern, his trousers clinging uncomfortably in places, and his shoes making squelching, sucking noises with every step.

He had never been much into caves — dirty, malodorous places the few he had explored — but this was an exception. The floor was of polished green stone with red flecks gleaming just beneath the surface. The walls were deeply scalloped and silver-grey, rising exceedingly high to a great spanning ceiling, much like polished granite but with cool, turquoise blue waves running through it; the whole chamber imbued with a kind of opulence and airiness entirely incongruent with something existing underground.

Underground — all that weight of earth and stone pressing down — a thought he would rather not entertain presently, lest the unthinkable happen and he were to be crushed in some freakish collapse, or worse, to be trapped in cold darkness without any hope of a rescue. To die a lone and lingering death. The mere idea sent a cold shiver along his spine, and he tried hard to push it as far from his mind as possible.

He had covered perhaps half the distance when something caught his eye. There appeared to be movement within the wall ahead, or was it some sort of illusion again? As he continued on, the faint strains of vaguely recognisable music reached his ears, the configuration of the capacious hollow making it difficult to tell exactly from which direction, but the obvious guess was that it emanated from the vicinity of the strange apparition he was headed towards, which, even at this distance, was beginning to look suspiciously like a pair of escalators.

"Am I in the basement of Buckley's and Nunn?" he intoned dryly to himself.

There was no doubt. It was indeed a pair of escalators – one travelled upwards, the other, down. His eyes held the curiosities as he covered the remaining distance, at last coming to a halt before them, standing in perusal of this latest dilemma, dripping wet.

Each shaft was long and dwindled into the distance without any visible end. He had already experienced the machine's crafty nature. Its predilection for enticing him on where better judgement might advise retreat. But retreat was not an option, regrettably.

Warily, he observed the moving stairways travel their opposite ways, ruing his miserable fortune in pushing his luck so far. For a little while he had been a winner. He had been three hundred and thirty dollars up before the machine had tricked him, and he had lost it all. If it hadn't tricked him, he would have won a bundle. Maybe two or three *thousand!*

"How do I know that one of these is really the right way? You've cheated me once already!"

In the air before him, appeared:

THERE IS NO WRONG WAY
EXIT IS ATTAINABLE FROM ANY
LOCATION WITHIN THE MAZE

"Exit? But you said there were two exits!"
ADDITIONAL EXIT AVAILABLE PENDING

REQUIRED LEVEL OF PARTICIPATION

He found the machine's unremitting manner unbearably annoying. "I wish you would stop repeating yourself," he rejoined. "It's very tiresome." Then, with renewed vigour: "You ruined my cigarettes, you tin-plated tyrant. You owe me a packet of cigarettes!"

YOU REQUIRE CIGARETTES?

"Yes. Didn't I just tell you?"

WHAT BRAND WOULD YOU LIKE?

This he had not expected. He dithered a moment. "Jackson Pollok," he expressed at last.

The air before John shivered as a small, rectangular window materialised, behind the window a metal compartment about the size of a shoe-box.

DEPOSIT NINE MONETARY UNITS HERE

"Are you kidding? You *owe me* the cigarettes. I ought to sue for endangering life and damage to personal property," he argued, indicating the condition of his clothes by tugging at them here and there. "What about that, huh?"

OMNICORP ACCEPTS NO
LIABILITY FOR ANY LOSS

"Omnicorp accepts no liability for any lose," he read, pitching his voice mockingly. And again for good measure: "Omnicorp accepts no liability for any loss.

"Get a life, you. . . vapid vending-machine. I don't care how long it takes, I'm not going on until you replace the cigarettes you ruined. I mean it this time. Not another step until you make good with the smokes."

The machine remained unresponsive, during which time John could have sworn he sensed an air of resentment — almost petulance. He wondered if perhaps he hadn't gone a tad too far with the *vapid vending- machine* crack. He was, after all, totally at the mercy of this this vapid vending machine.

With a tiny flicker of light, a packet of Jackson Pollok appeared inside the metal compartment.

YOUR CIGARETTES ARE AVAILABLE

"And I should think so, too," he chortled victoriously. Flipping back the window he took possession of his prize.

While he considered which pocket to put them in, he asked, "If I find the exit, what do I win? You haven't told me that yet."

GAINING EXIT VIA SHORTEST ROUTE
WINS 10,000 MONETARY UNITS

PROPORTIONATE SUM AWARDED
ACCORDING TO DISTANCE TRAVELLED

FAILURE TO DISCOVER EXIT WILL
PRECIPITATE FORFEITURE OF YOUR
INITIAL INVESTMENT SUM

ONE MONETARY UNIT

"And one monetary unit is a dollar, right?"

YES

"Hmm," he expressed, considering. Ten thousand smackers. It's certainly a tidy sum. Perhaps his predicament was not quite so hopeless as he had imagined. The immediate problem was simple enough: Did he want to ride the up escalator, or the down escalator?

Being underground made him uneasy — all that massive weight pressing down — and besides, the exit couldn't be down here. Where was there to exit to?

"All right," he announced to the cavern walls. "Let's see what kind of a maze this is." He stepped forward onto the rising escalator.

He had travelled only a dozen metres or so when the piped music being fed into the shaft ceased, recommencing shortly afterwards with a tune he recognised at once, a tenuously scored version of *Fool on the Hill.* He didn't like this at all. Misgivings rose swiftly. That the music was merely part of a random selection was doubtful. The machine was far too calculating for that, he had already learned. He turned and, with all the speed he could muster, took flight, negotiating the stairs two and three at a time in a desperate bid to reach the relative safety of the cavern below.

The distance was not great, just twenty metres or so. Neither was the escalator's speed rapid. He made good ground, gaining ten metres rather more easily than he expected, but then his heel caught on a riser as his wet and clinging trousers hindered his stride, sending him sprawling, headlong down the steps.

His ribs took the brunt of the fall, but his knee struck a sharp edge which produced exquisite pain, and for a while he lay in a tangle, wincing, trying to assess the extent of his injuries. No time even for that he realised at once. With every passing second carrying him further along, he scrambled desperately to his feet and took up the chase anew.

He had lost all of the ten metres he had previously gained, maybe more, and his knee was beginning to stiffen from the heavy knock. Even though, he was making headway, and he kept up the struggle, doubling his effort in noticing his gradual advance. All of the while the plaintive rendition of *Fool on the Hill* sounding in his ears, striking a fearful chord in him as his eyes held a determined focus on the base of the shaft.

Nearer — he was coming nearer. Just five or six metres more, but he was tiring, his legs growing weaker with every stride, and his breathing came now in short, ragged gasps. Months of idleness were taking their toll. All those cigarettes, the beers and fat-laden meals. Even six months ago he might have made it, but his morning constitutional had a good while ago been abandoned in favour of coffee and a cigarette; a crossword-puzzle at the kitchen table.

Exhaustion finally claimed him and he was forced to give up the vain pursuit. Inexplicably, the voice of his wife filled the shaft. "You're shiftless, John Edwards. Totally shiftless. You'll be dead of a heart attack before forty-five at this rate. You heed my words. Before forty-five."

He slumped against the smooth panelling of the escalator, wheezing. Battered and beaten, his lungs working hard to replenish spent oxygen. "Oh sh-ut u-up," he managed, in barely a whisper. "Sh-ut the h-hell up."

A full minute elapsed before he was able to give some attention to his injuries. He lifted his trouser leg, revealing a goodly sized dent in his shin and a dark bruise developing. Higher up, blood trickled from a small cut in his knee where he had caught the edge of a stair. Of no particular consequence, he judged, and lifted his wind-cheater to uncover some minor scrapes and bruises there.

"I guess I'll live," he told himself despondently, and looked up to see what appeared to be the end of the ride. He pushed himself to his feet and peered nervously ahead.

Where the escalator seemed to terminate, the roof continued to rake upwards, fanning out wide and creating a large open space. The landing platform must, therefore, be just beyond the top of the incline, he reasonably assumed. But, no — nothing!

With his heart in his mouth he stared disbelievingly out, into the open air into which this fiendish mechanism meant to deliver him.

He turned in readiness to run, knowing full well there was no chance of escape, and in doing so a current of pain from his injured knee brought him down. Unable to rise again, terror swept over him, and all he was able to do, he did.

A breath away from the edge of the prodigious drop, he screamed, long and loud — a primal and instinctive expurgation of fear and frustration, and in defiance of this terrible and unrelenting unreality. . . .

With a sense of relief so great that it numbed his mind, the horrendous launch failed to eventuate. Where he had expected to be plummeting to an ignoble and certain end, without so much as a bump, he was carried over the apex and sharply downwards, surrounded now by nothing at all except for the escalator rails on either side oh him. He was precariously poised in near a vertical descent.

Too shaken to think, for a time his single concern was with maintaining his perilous position on the too narrow perch of an escalator riser. Only after gasping for breath did he realise he had been doing this to the exclusion of all else. Arms stretched out horizontally, and with white-knuckled purchase on the rails either side, he gazed down into the emptiness where, in the far, far distance, the escalator dwindled away until it vanished from sight.

A new tune now issued pervasively from the unknown source, proving a noisome distraction as he concentrated hard on staying put. Hardly unobtrusive when your whole universe consisted of only one's self and the ability to sit still, the painfully simple melody took on ubiquitous proportions.

"*Girl from* bloody *Ipanema*," he moaned through clenched teeth.

Time passed lingeringly and uneventfully — twenty minutes and more — and still the steady descent. Still the same, mindnumbingly bland music, repeated without pause or the slightest variation.

"It can't last forever," he told himself, feigning conviction.

Holding on to the side rails any longer became impossible. Both his shoulders and arms had begun to ache so severely that he was forced to devise an alternative means of securing himself. After a moment of hesitation, he released his grip and lowered his arms, and sitting stiffly upright, took a firm hold of the ledge beneath him. There was another major drawback involved in sitting for so long on furrowed metal. To relieve the growing discomfort lower down, he adjusted his position, ever so slightly, for fear of toppling forward.

"I can wait," he muttered, accompanied by a grimace.

After a further ten minutes he reached into his pocket, taking pains to move no more than was absolutely necessary. From the pocket he pulled out the packet of Jackson Pollok. Tearing away the cellophane wrapper with his teeth, he likewise coaxed a cigarette from the pack, but as he patted his pockets searchingly, a look of bitter realisation came upon his face. . . On the ledge beside the machine. . !

"My damned cigarette lighter, you over-blown pinballmachine."

YOUR LIGHTER IS UNAVAILABLE DO
YOU REQUIRE A REPLACEMENT?

"Yes, I require a replacement!"

In the same manner as before, a small rectangular window materialised in front of him. "And don't dare be asking me to pay for it."

AS YOU WISH

Behind the window appeared a splendid-looking cigarette-lighter, similar in design to his cheap disposable but with a nacreous finish, and trimmed in a gold-coloured metal with the Omnicorp logo emblazoned on each side.

He accepted it somewhat petulantly, regarding it with grudging appreciation before lighting his cigarette.

"And stop that God-awful music. Better still, get me off this diabolical contraption!"

GAME IN PROGRESS_PROGRAM UNALTERABLE

The little window winked out of sight, apparently signifying an end to the exchange.

"How much longer am I expected to endure this?" he called. There was no response.

"Damn you. Where are you taking me?"

Compulsively, and in long-accustomed fashion, he drew deeply on his cigarette, exhaled slowly and evenly in effort to counter mounting vexation... and waited. There was nothing to be done but keep a firm grip until he was delivered to whatever destination this uncanny conveyance was taking him to.

Down and down and down... Time passed without any event by which to mark its passage. There was only the continuous, dull inactivity; sitting, waiting apprehensively for something to occur, and all-the-while played the tenuous melody, unsettling and grating the nerves.

He considered putting his fingers in his ears, and would have but for it requiring that he let go his grip.

As an alternative he plugged his ears with cigarettes; the filters serving the purpose exceptionally well — so well in fact that he had to remove them when the silence became a problem.

When further forbearance seemed impossible, he took to singing loudly what few songs he knew. When every song had been sung twice over, still the excruciating melody persisted.

He peered down in front of him, along the endless escalator to where it disappeared in a pin-point amid nothingness.

"I'm in hell," he said to himself in a half-whisper. "What can I do?"

There was nothing he could do — no action he could take which might reasonably be expected to release him from his frightful predicament. Exerting grim self-control, *and absently reaching for another cigarette*, he endeavoured to steer his thoughts toward some relieving diversion in a bid to keep panic from gaining the upper hand.

As a ship unleashed from its moorings, of its own volition his mind drifted back to a period in his life which had escaped any prior reflection. The aberration immediately struck him as being a curious phenomenon. That he had not once looked back on it since its occurrence was wonder enough, but the clarity now — after all this time

— the ease with which every detail was remembered — every sight, sound and odour, impressing itself in a way that augmented even the original experience.

He was twenty two years old at the time, and it was in the autumn. He had made a decision spurred by the strange compulsion to isolate himself, taking up residence in an upstairs annex by the coast, many miles from family and friends. His intention had been to apply himself to his *then* great passion of painting, and to this place he had hurried, amply supplied with canvasses, oil-colours and every conceivable accessory, ready to embark on a new way of life, free of all distraction, every care or concern.

The memory began with John standing alone in the front room, he stood before the first blank canvass in anticipation of the arrival of the necessary inspiration. Beyond the window, with curtains tied far back for access to light, a panorama of coastline sea and sky stretched away expansively. For a long time he remained in contemplation of what might be his first serious work, summoning images and colour schemes of great sophistication, visualising masterpieces; perhaps universal acclaim, until the moment was lost and the room began to crowd in on him. A stroll along the foreshore and a take-away meal brought the day to a close.

At dawn he rose, his enthusiasm already waning and the first murmuring voices of doubt creeping in. In the pale light, tentative brushstrokes were made, expressing some inner discontent rather than depicting any clear idea, and as the day grew brighter so did endeavour and perseverance subside.

Two hours before dawn on the following day, he again took up the task. Unshaven, unwashed, his clothes creased and misshapen from long hours spent huddled on the couch, he bent to his work with gathering momentum, becoming so intensely absorbed that, for a time he felt reality yield — bend as if it were something pliable — giving way to a realm of experience subjective and self- generated, until the full light of day penetrated to the corners of the room and brought an end to the spell.

He started again at around midnight, the beginning of the fourth day, having discovered that only the hours of darkness were conducive to the creative energy now wholly at work, lending quiet solitude by which the mind's inner workings were able to focus intensely enough to begin the process of translating subject to tangible form . . . and time slipped by unnoticed in the feverish haze of pursuit.

Hours later — how long was impossible to tell — damp with sweat and eyes blazing with creative fervour, the activity ceased abruptly. Palettes and brushes were thrown to the floor as if, at last, he had released himself from an intolerable burden, and stepping back shakily he stood in contemplative repose.

In his face weariness mingled with surprise, as though, only now, he were seeing it for the first time. Surprise changed to astonishment, then quickly to a mixture of disbelief and repugnance as recognised elements within the composition revealed themselves to him. In fearful response he snatched up his jacket and fled into the brightness of the day.

Until noon he walked south along the shoreline before resting. At dusk he returned to the township, on impulse purchasing a quart of whiskey before returning to sit on the couch and stare at the strange, unnerving vision he had captured: From within the canvas, eyes staring back. Not on or from the canvass, but *within*.

There was a delicate, swirling mist of greys and blues entwined. Turbid suffusions where shape, shadow and light fragmented, baffling the eye and veiling all in palpable uncertainty. Half-seen shapes lurked there and, a creature, large, dark, indistinct; its form perceived more through mere sense of presence than actual depiction, waiting broodingly, just inside the mist. And its eyes. . .

With a jolt John returned to the present, astounded by the memory which for so long had remained locked away in some deep recess, only now to be conjured in so haunting and vivid a fashion. Yes, I wanted to be an artist, he remembered wistfully; and he remembered, too, the alcohol- induced delirium which had consumed him that night, marking the place in his life where his dream of being an artist had been forever dashed, a harbinger of dark times, heralding the protracted bout of melancholy that followed.

He drew heavily on his cigarette, willing the memory gone, and exhaled. The smoke plumed outward and billowed into a cloud which hung about him, rolling gently. It was a little while before he noticed this, but then his brow furrowed.

His motion ought to be carrying him away from the smoke, yet it hung in the air around him. Was he still descending? The passing panels at the sides of the escalator implied that he *was*, although the fact that he was surrounded by lingering smoke stood in stark contradiction.

He flicked the cigarette butt away as he pondered the curiosity, and to his acute surprise it vanished, mid-air, less than a metre from where he sat.

"What the—!" Uttered in astonishment.

Ensuring safe purchase on the hand-rail he carefully rose and moved down a step. Now he was close to where the butt had disappeared, but peering as hard as he could, provided no clue.

One step more, he told himself. Gingerly he slid his foot forwards. When the toe of his boot disappeared he let out an involuntary yelp and withdrew, pausing a moment before gathering enough courage to try again.

Resisting the impulse not to, he forced his foot and then his leg beyond the invisible border, discovering solid footing on the other side,

and battling against fast-rising trepidation he stepped through...

...into darkness. Utter, cloistering, terrible: causing immediate disorientation such that, already, he found it impossible to determine from which direction he had entered. Logic advised a backward step, which did nothing but upset his balance, and in panic he dropped to hug the floor... at that moment the one physical certainty in the universe.

There was a sensation of rising - a force being exerted from beneath, not unlike that of a lift gaining momentum - and suddenly there was light. He looked up to find himself lying on the floor of a small, octagonal- shaped compartment, the light source, like that of the underground cavern, undetectable but wholly adequate.

On the eight sides of the compartment, eight landscape scenes were displayed behind glass screens, including forests, mountainous country which looked very inhospitable, and one which could easily pass for the lunar surface. He didn't much like the look of any of them, but he climbed to his feet to take a closer look.

A voice, neither male nor female in quality, said:

"Choose a destination by placing palm against the screen applicable. Refreshments are available through voice command." Had he thought it would achieve anything, John would have demanded a halt to this madness, but the offer of refreshment did go some way to diverting his attention. The last, lingering effect of the alcohol he had consumed was an exceedingly dry mouth.

"Water," he said, though he very nearly ordered a beer, and on a ledge before him appeared a jug of water and a glass.

He drank one glass straight down and poured himself another. "How much longer is this going to continue?"

"Alternative exit will become available after next stage," came the perfunctory reply.

"And the alternative exit is. . . ?" "Alternative," the voice responded.

He sipped the water and began to study the picture panels, taking pains to try and judge such things as climate, ease of passage and overall pleasantness. After looking carefully at each one here turned to stand in front of the rural landscape, the least worrisome of all, he felt.

"All right then," he said, squaring his shoulders. "A stroll in the country it is." And, so saying, he pressed his palm to the screen, the result being not quite what he had expected.

He found himself standing in a picture gallery. A polished timber floor and high white walls hung with numerous artworks. A high curved ceiling on which the night sky was represented in amazing detail — every constellation clearly recognisable. In front of him hung the rural scene he had expected to enter.

"Son of a bitch," he muttered angrily, at once understanding the ruse. "Now what?"

LOCATE EXIT

DURATION AND DISTANCE TRAVELLED TO BE FACTORED INTO POINT SCORE TOTALISATION

"That wasn't what I meant. And, anyway, it was a rhetorical question, you deplorable sneak!"

The message faded out and he looked in both directions along the very large room.

At both ends, and midway on both sides, were high archways. But, which way to go? As far as that went, he realised that without any clue there was little to be considered. So then luck would have to provide.

He set off towards the nearest archway which was situated about fifty metres along the near wall. Casting a casual eye over some of the exhibits as he went, he was impressed by the quality of the images held within the frames. Holograms all, he determined, but far superior to any hologram he had ever seen. It appeared that this room was given over to the theme of *big*, including man-made structures and geographical features like the Great Wall, the pyramids of Gizeh, Everest and Uluru, all captured with such clarity that it was just like viewing the real thing, observed from some optimum vantage-point. But, then, coming upon what he recognised as Victoria Falls, he halted. The mile-wide Zambezi plummeted into the deep gorge throwing up a fine, dense mist in which refracted light swirled in shifting colours.

Was it possible these were just what they appeared to be, after all — windows into actual locations? If his present situation been other than what it was he might have allowed himself the time to stand in wonder, but this being far from a leisurely stroll through a municipal gallery, he pressed on.

Passing through the archway he entered a room of identical dimensions. On the ceiling, as with the previous room, a galactic vista, this time quite unrecognisable however, and a glance at a nearby exhibit told why.

It captured an elevated view of a city: tall towers and sleek spires of emerald green and ruby red, glistening beneath a pale yellow sun. On top of a barren hill, overlooking the jagged skyline, sat a gargantuan sculpture of a winged beast which he thought most resembled a dog, although scaly and, where ears might have been, it had short, pointy horns. It reared, with a long whiplike tail snaking behind and powerful forelegs outstretched, raking the air with single claws as long as a man's arm. Its head was its most canine feature, with rows of long teeth exposed in a snarl, and its eyes, staring up to the mauve-coloured sky, seemed full of torment, its wings, though frozen in depiction, easily imagined to be lashing wildly about, raising a great cloud of dust into the air.

The sculpture made him feel decidedly uneasy. Not because of the strangeness of the beast, but quite irrationally, the image stirred vague feelings of loss and desolation, unpleasant sensations which were best left to lie undisturbed. He turned from the exhibit and with renewed purpose, strode off towards the adjoining room.

Room after room he traversed without letting himself be diverted, however exotic or enticing the works on display. His strategy was simple. If he walked in one direction for long enough, it had to lead him somewhere, and with this single thought in mind he followed a straight line that dissected each room through their central archways.

After perhaps ten minutes of this, confidence in the strategy had already begun to erode. To make matters worse the tune which had plagued him for so long on the escalator was now, even more annoyingly playing inside his head. When he caught himself humming along, he began to search his mind for something of a distracting nature. Perhaps it was the white walls. Some perceived similarity in the architecture that gave rise to a long-forgotten memory.

Fargo Hospital had been where his reawakening to the real world had taken place. Dimly at first, then gradually with greater connection and substance, things had begun to make sense again; though never in quite the same way as before.

A nervous breakdown. Not an uncommon manifestation when stress, poor diet and alcohol were in combination, the doctor had told him. And the creature in the painting? Well, the mind was inclined to play tricks under such conditions.

John halted at the centre of the room. He hadn't been counting, but he had passed through a good many rooms and his legs were beginning to get tired. He stood for a moment in consideration, finally deciding that a change in direction might, at least, result in some form of relief from the boring repetition he was having to endure. As he set off towards one end of the room at a slightly more leisurely pace, he let his attention stray to the exhibits, discovering now a major difference in subject matter.

Where previously still life or landscape had been the subject, here there was activity, and organised activity at that! Within one frame a polychromatic fluid moved slowly and freely, without any apparent purpose, then gaining speed rapidly it executed precise, intricate manoeuvres before separating into individual colours and mixed hues, exploding into three- dimensional configurations of fantastic complexity. If these were meant to be representational of anything, he had no way of knowing, but the process was fascinating and intriguing to observe as, in around every eight seconds, it was repeated to produce new and equally spectacular arrangements.

He had the strange feeling that he was witnessing this fluid seek self expression, maybe even some kind of identity, yet never being able to maintain the one form for more than this transient moment. The notion was, of course, absurd. He realised it was just his own interpretation, but, still, he couldn't help feeling a little saddened by the thought of such a vain and fruitless struggle.

Much of what he saw defied comprehension, but further along the way he encountered something not quite so mystifying. The exhibit consisted of two oblong windows or panels. In the first, standing at the centre of a valley between two mountains, a submarine city beneath a huge, transparent dome. The city's architecture was blockish and utilitarian, this to some degree compensated for by decorative murals on many of the walls. Where an area had been picturesquely transformed into parkland, what may well have been communication-towers reached up. Tall and slender frameworks, glistening like crystalline stalagmites with gossamerlike fans spreading out half-circle at their tops.

From the centre of the city three colour-tinted, transparent tubes rose outward at a gentle angle, passing through the protective dome and on, but lost to view at the edge of the frame. At the edge of the adjacent window, these same tubes rose out of the ocean and continued into the heart of a coastal metropolis. As he watched, he noticed some kind of vehicle moving within, departing the limits of the city and accelerating rapidly towards the shoreline, there disappearing beneath the surface of the water.

John turned and resumed walking towards the end archway, wondering at the significance, if any, of what he saw. Was it merely fanciful invention, some contrived conception of art? If not, what the hell was he witnessing here? The question stayed with him as he passed beneath the archway and stepped into a forest glade.

With the sudden and unexpected transition he froze, mid-stride, then spun about in vain hope of finding the way back. It wasn't there as he knew it wouldn't be. He was standing at the centre of the glade, dense forest encircling and three pathways leading into it, his feet at their intersection. Bright sunlight lit the grassy expanse, green, golden and lush. Before him the dappled shadows reached out, indicating the time of day to be late afternoon.

"All right, that's it. I want out of here," he yelled to the tranquil surroundings.

ALTERNATIVE EXIT IS NOW AVAILABLE

"And about flamin' time, too! So, where is it?"

YOU ARE DOING FINE WHY NOT CONTINUE?

"I don't want to continue. I've had enough, you hear me? Enough!"

EARLY EXIT REQUIRES POINT
SCORE FORFEITURE

"What?" He paused for a moment, remembering his loss on the game of Recall. "Okay, fine. Do it."

YOUR CURRENT SCORE IS ZERO

"Exactly. Just what you deserve, you automated swindler. Now get me out of here!"

CREDIT EXTENDED

1 ALCOHOLIC BEVERAGE: 10 monetary units
1 PHENOGLYPH TRANSLATION: 5 monetary units
1 PACKET OF CIGARETTES: 9 monetary units 1
DELUXE CIGARETTE LIGHTER: 95 monetary units
1 JUG OF MINERAL SPRING WATER: 1 monetary unit
TOTAL:120 monetary units

DO YOU WISH TO SETTLE OUTSTANDING DEBT AND TAKE EARLY EXIT OPPORTUNITY NOW?

John's heart sank. "You can't possibly. How can you...? You bastard," he protested feebly.

GOODS SUPPLIED UPON REQUEST
ONLY IN EXCHANGE FOR PAYMENT
OMNICORP ACCEPTS NO LIABILITY

He lowered himself to sit on the soft grass, fatigue and despair thwarting his efforts for clear thought. "I'm a goner," he groaned.

GAME IN PROGRESS

"I'm done for."

He looked despondently around him. He wished that he was home, even with all the problems and responsibilities that included. And he missed his baby daughter. He pictured her at this moment, lying asleep in her cot, her plump little face so innocent and free of any cares.

THIS FACILITY HAS BEEN AUTHORISED BY OMNICORP TO PROVIDE YOU WITH A LIMITED CREDIT OPTION
conditions apply

"What does that mean?"

A LOAN

"You'll lend me the money to buy my way out?"

YES

"Go unscrew yourself," he retorted, taking offence. "I've not borrowed a cent in ten years, and I'm not about to start now."

AS YOU WISH

"This is absurd," he said to himself. "I'm actually being held to ransom by a bloody game machine. "Extortion!" he yelled to the sky. "That's what this is, bloody extortion! It's a crime where I come from, you know!" He stood suddenly, a look of new-found determination in his face, and choosing one of the three paths, he set off along it.

Distance was deceiving, perhaps because of the rapidly lengthening shadows, and the edge of the forest drew little nearer for his effort. He kept on, stubbornly, not to be daunted by any further chicanery, broadening his stride as outright defiance spurred him on.

Breathing hard, he at last reached the verge of the forest, red-faced with anger and hypertension, and there the trail ended in a tangle of undergrowth. Peering into the gloom, his vision penetrated only a few metres before meeting with total darkness. The sky, too, was fast fading of all colour.

In frustration he barged forward, only to be thrown back by the undergrowth, tough and somewhat elastic in nature, which enraged him all the more. Readying himself for another attempt, the sound of footfalls, soft but heavy-sounding, came out of the deeper murk. Then came a low growl which turned him cold and raised the hair on the back of his neck. Primal fear carried him faster than he had moved in years, back in the direction he had come from, with frequent, terrified glances over his shoulder, in fear of what might have been following.

Darkness had claimed the glade by the time he returned to the intersection of pathways, and there he let himself collapse to the grass in exhaustion, to lay panting and looking up into the dark sky.

No stars, he noticed — though not for some time. His body felt leaden, his limbs, rubbery. His lungs burned like mad and he feared his heart was about to fail. The sky was as black as tar and out of its inky depths images pressed in on him:

The brightness of the delivery room and people dressed in surgical gowns ... the peeling green paint on the nursery walls and long periods alone ... a blue tricycle ... a cowboy costume ... school- yards ... sunshine and the childish exaltations of life ... a future unclouded by doubt or misgivings ... standing beside his father's freshly covered grave ... his mother reading from the *Book of Psalms* as large drops of rain disturbed the dry dust ... day- labouring at the wharves ... his first car, bought with money scrimped and saved ... Carla, the movies ... Lioni, restaurants ... Denise, weekend outings ... the first sweet pangs of young love ... a sudden, unaccountable change ... moodiness ... brooding discontent ... distrust of people and the need for seclusion.

Rustling in the grass brought him out of his deep reflection. In the darkness, footsteps approached. Fear gripped him and he jumped to his feet, straining hard to detect the faintest of sounds, but now there was nothing. The night had become deathly still, charged with an unnatural energy that made his skin crawl and his scalp tingle. Black within blackness, something moved, and the pure stench of evil cloyed his senses.

"No! Stay away," he called desperately. "Get me out. Oh please, please, get me out!"

LOAN OPTION STILL AVAILABLE "Yes. All right!" COLLATERAL IS REQUIRED DO YOU OWN YOUR OWN HOME?

"No, not the house, you bastard!" He grew frantic, sensing whatever it was out there drawing ever nearer.

COLLATERAL IS REQUIRED

"Oh, God, it's coming!" he wailed, distraught with terror. "Not the house. Anything, but not the house!"

IT IS AGREED

PLEASE PRESS PALM TO RECORDING
PANEL FOR HAND PRINT RATIFICATION

So dark as to cause the night to pale in comparison, something large and lithe loomed closer. Eyes, smouldering red and set wide apart pierced the grey penumbra... and came a growl so low and menacing that his insides trembled in terrible resonance to it.

PLEASE PRESS PALM TO RECORDING PANEL

Indistinct, just beyond the bounds of sight, it circled with ill intent. From the ground rose a blue-grey mist, rolling and swirling, spilling away from its passage as a bow wave before a large vessel. Other half-seen shapes emerged, moving stealthily within the mist which rapidly filled with tiny coalescing points of blue light, casting no light at all.

PRESS PALM TO RECORDING PANEL

He stood transfixed by fear, but this time the ethereal message was reinforced by a calm, commanding voice that seemed to emanate from within his head. He responded slowly, afraid that any quicker movement might provoke an attack by the fearsome creature of his id whose cold gaze he felt pierce him to the core.

With his hand about to make contact with the panel, the creature let out a shriek so awful that it felt to tear his very fibre and was dreadful to endure. Terror stricken beyond tolerance and screaming, he forced his hand the last few centimetres until contact was made with the panel.

He was still screaming at the top of his lungs as he appeared on a vast, red plain beneath azure sky. Inexplicably, all sense of fear and dread had gone, and so relieved was he to be out of the nightmarish predicament, and feeling like a complete fool, he ceased from screaming. Evidently, though, he was not yet out of the game.

GAME CANCELLED

SELECTION 4: 4. MAZESCORE: 0

GAME SELECTION

1. FRUIT	0	4. MAZE	0	7. QUANDARY	x1
2. TAROT	x10	5. PORTALS	x5	8. ILLUSION	x10
3. WHEEL	330	6. RECALL	-325	9. CHANCE	x1

GAME 4. EXIT FEE: -10

GOODS AND SERVICES PROVIDED: -120
LOAN OPTION ACTIVATED: 130
monetary units AGGREGATE: 0

LOAN SETTLEMENT PENDING GAME
OUTCOME INSERT ONE MONETARY
UNIT AND TRY AGAIN

"You've cheated me again," he said, still surprised by how calm he felt. "The exit fee, you crook! I can't believe it."

GAME 4 HAS BEEN EXITED AS AGREED
COMPLETION OF ALL SELECTIONS REQUIRED
TO DERIVE AGGREGATE POINT SCORE

"Screw aggregate point score totalisation! I want to go home!"

OPERATIONAL GUIDANCE IS A FEATURE
OF THE SERIES FIVE ALPHA FACILITY

"Meaning?"

DO YOU REQUIRE ASSISTANCE?
"From you? Why would I drop a scorpion down my shorts?"

AN INTERESTING METAPHOR BASED
ON AN ERRONEOUS ASSUMPTION

OPERATIONAL GUIDANCE IS MERELY A
USER-FRIENDLY FEATURE INCLUDED FOR
YOUR CONVENIENCE IN THE SELECTION-
MAKING PROCESS   NOTHING MORE

DO YOU WISH TO TAKE ADVANTAGE
OF THIS FEATURE?

He thought it over for a while, carefully. "How much will it cost me?"

OPERATIONAL GUIDANCE INCURS NO CHARGE

"Well...okay. I don't suppose it could do any harm. What do I do?"

ASK YOUR QUESTION

"Oh," he responded, irritated and feeling slightly foolish. "How do I get out of here? And I do NOT mean just out of *here*."

He indicated his present surroundings."How do I get back home?"

FROM THIS JUNCTURE THERE
ARE TWO POSSIBILITIES

1.   COMPLETE GAME SCHEDULE
2.   SELECT CHANCE

CHANCE SELECTION PROVIDES SCHEDULED PROGRAM EXIT, STANDARD TO ALL ALPHA SERIES FACILITIES.

"You're not bullshitting me?" Excitement rising in anticipation of imminent liberty.

ONNICORP GAMING FACILITIES ARE SUBJECT TO STRINGENT GUIDELINES SET DOWN BY THE UNIVERSAL GAMBLING AUTHORITY. . .BULLSHITTING IS NOT PERMITTED AND CARRIES A HEAVY PENALTY

John was thoughtful for a time, then replied, "Well, I guess it's okay then. All right. I'll try this chance thing, I suppose."

INSERT ONE MONETARY UNIT

When the coin-slot appeared before him, he groaned peevishly, but resignedly searched his pockets for a dollar coin. As far as he knew, his coin cup, still with three dollars in it, sat on the ledge in front of this diabolical machine.

He remembered the remains of the shopping money — twenty- six dollars, if he remembered correctly — and unfolding his wallet he found just that amount, the gold coin wedged in a corner of the small pocket.

Returning the wallet to his hip pocket John stood with the coin held ready. "Not much choice, really," he muttered sullenly, and dropped the coin into the slot.

GAME SELECTION

1. FRUIT	0	4. MAZE	0	7. QUANDARY	x1
2. TAROT	x10	5. PORTALS	x5	8. ILLUSION	x1
3. WHEEL	330	6. RECALL	-325	9. CHANCE	x1

TO MAKE SELECTION

STATE GAME TITLE AND CORRESPONDING NUMBER

"Chance. Number nine," he said, managing to keep his voice steady. Now he was confined in a small room constructed of roughly hewn blocks of grey stone, lit by two flickering torches mounted on opposite walls. Under the flickering illumination he noticed that the floor was blue-grey in colour and perfectly smooth, without any detectable imperfection, which lent a certain incongruity to the scene. In one shadowy corner an iron wrought stand supported a wooden tub, a ladle hanging from a wooden peg above it. From behind, a thin, wavery voice surprised him.

"What are you doing here?" it said.

He spun, eyes wide and searching, to find that there was someone lying on a pile of straw in the corner. That someone was dressed in rags and supinely reposed, with a stale-looking, half eaten loaf of bread resting on his stomach. An old man, pale and thin, with long white hair and beard, and dark, beady little eyes which glistened in the torchlight.

"I said, what are you doing here?" he repeated in his querulous tone.

"Who are you?"

"I asked first," the old man insisted. "I don't know what I'm doing here."

"Then you ain't too bright, are you?" The old man looked John up and down while he scratched under his shaggy whiskers. "Can't stay here," he said.

"Why would I want to?" "Can't anyway. No room."

John made a deliberate examination of the room, drawing special attention to the fact that there was no apparent way of leaving. At this, the old man began to chuckle. A response John found most annoying.

"What the hell are you cackling about, old man?"

"Don't you go cussin' me. I ain't the one that came buttin' in on you, am I. You ain't been here five minutes and already you causin' trouble."

John looked suitably chastened.

"Goddamn it," the old man expressed in frustration."As if things ain't bad enough." He fell to dejected silence.

John stood awaiting further reproof. None came, but as time continued to stretch on, the silence was becoming uncomfortable.

"I'm sorry," he said at last, "but it's not my fault that I'm here." The old man began to laugh again while John watched bemusedly, with a look on his face betraying the uncomfortable realisation that he might be locked in a room with a madman.

The old man's laughter ceased abruptly. "You really are stupid, aren't you, boy. It's not my fault I'm here," he mimicked sarcastically.

"Well, who the damn hell's fault is it?" John made no reply.

"You dummy. Of course it's your fault. Some bright specimen, eh?" he said, as if to someone beside him.

"I wish you wouldn't keep on insulting me. It seems we're trapped here together. At least we could try to get on."

"It seems, does it? Does it really? It seems?"

John tried to ignore the man's rancour. He walked over to the wooden tub to see what it contained, and was hit in the back of the head by the half-loaf of stale bread.

"Keep away from there. That's my water. You can't stay here." "All right, all right. Calm down, I was only looking."

He came back to stand in the middle of the room. "You want to tell me how I can leave?"

"You took a chance. Your chance will come," he said, a sly glint in his eyes. "Yes, that's right, I know. You needn't look so surprised. How do you think I got here? And I ain't sayin' this is so bad," he quickly added, glancing apprehensively towards the stone ceiling. "This ain't so bad at all. Seen worse — much worse."

"Who are you talking to?" John asked, following his line of sight. "Shhhh," the old man hissed, pressing a finger to his lips. With surprising speed he got up and ran over to John, grabbing hold of an arm and speaking close to his ear. "Don't go drawing attention. You don't want to do that," he warned.

"The machine, you mean?"

"Noooo!" The old man became distraught. "No! No! No! No!"

He clutched his ears and ran back to the corner to fall into the pile straw.

"Don't say its name. Don't draw attention." He moaned and writhed around for a while before falling silent. After a brief lull he raised his head. "Yes, that's exactly what I mean, you idiot."

"Look," John began angrily. "I'm thoroughly fed up of you-" But the old man cut him off, asking, "How old would you say I am? Go on, have a guess. How old?"

John let it pass. He didn't like being angry anyway. Shrugging, he guessed, "Seventy-two?"

"Oh – Right. Seventy-two," he replied, obviously disappointed that John had guessed correctly. "Well at least I was, you know, before…"

"Before you played the-"

"Shhhh!" The old man prevented him from uttering the word, but nodded his head vigorously. "Yes. And who knows how long ago that was?"

"You don't know how long you've been here?"

"Ain't been so long," he replied, looking about insouciantly. "This ain't nothin'. This is beer and skittles, boy, compared to some of it. John looked around once more. "If you say so."

"I do say so," came the indignant reply. "You reckon I don't know what's good for me?"

"This," John said with arms spread wide, "is good for you?" "Could be worse." He looked about him as if to be sure no one was within earshot. "You seen them little critters, all teeth and claws, little bitty eyes what glow in the dark?"

John's eyes widened with interest. "No."

The old man snorted derisively. "You will. That's how I lost this arm," he said, raising a perfectly good arm. "Flesh-eating little blighters."

"But your arm isn't damaged," John pointed out. "You callin' me a liar?"

"No," he appeased.

"Shows how much you know," said the old man, calming somewhat. "You ain't been 'round long. Still a greenhorn, and not too bright besides."

John took a threatening pace forwards, fists clenched in anger and frustration.

"Ooh, nice, that is. You going to beat up on an old man, are you? An old man you break in on and steal his water and call him a liar in his own home. That what you young folks is like these days? No respect for the elderly?"

"Shut up. I'm not going to hurt you, okay? Cantankerous old goat," he finished, quietly.

"I heard that."

John took to wandering around the room.

"You can't stay here," said the old man once more, and he hunkered down in his bed of straw, watching the intruder through slitted eyes.

John circled the room three times before halting. He had noted everything worthy of note, which totalled nothing, and was at a loss to know what to do next. Withdrawing his cigarettes he paused and looked over to the old man. "You want a smoke?"

"You ain't lightin' one of those things up in here, boy. Not in my place you ain't."

John struggled with the dilemma, at last returning the cigarette to the packet. "I wonder how long this is going to take," he said musingly.

From his huddle, the old man replied sagely, "Don't be in too much of a hurry, boy. You're safe here, anyways."

"Can you tell me what to expect?" John asked levelly.

"No way of tellin'. Different every time. Some make it, some don't, I reckon."

"There's been others?"

"You ain't the first by a long shot. Seen all sorts. They come and they go."

"So what are you still doing here?"

"This'll do me. I like it here. And I know what you're thinkin', that the old boy is crazy. Well that may be, but I got no hankerin' to leave, and that's all I'm sayin' on the subject. Here it comes, dummy."

He was about to ask here comes what? when what became evident. One wall began to shimmer, the stone blocks merging into one flat surface, then turning liquid and changing colour to palest lilac. Now there was no wall at all, only a lilac expanse meeting a pale grey sky at a distant horizon.

Two stone arches materialised in the foreground. Beside each stood a creature of humanoid form, large of body and small of head, wearing helmets with visors pulled down so that their faces were hidden, chain mail and armour over massive bodies, and both clutching halberds at their sides.

"This looks good," said the old man. "Never seen this before."

CHANCE

THROUGH ONE GATE LIES HOME
THROUGH ONE THE UNKNOWN

BUT HERE IS THE CLUE

TWO QUESTIONS ONLY BEFORE
YOU DECIDE THE ONE OF THE TWO
COMMITTED TO LIES ONE TELLS YOU
TRUE YET HOW WILL YOU KNOW

WITHOUT ART IN THE ASKING
WHICH WAY TO GO

John's expression turned grave as the importance of the choice confronting him impressed itself on him.

"Oooo! This *is* a good one," the old man chirped gleefully.

"Shut up," John snapped, managing to quieten him to a subdued titter.

"Two questions. One committed to lies," he said to himself, trying to get it clear in his mind. "One will lie and the other will tell the truth."

He eyed the identical pair of sentinels with suspicion, and it dawned on him then, the dread consequence of letting an unintentional question slip past his lips. His knees weakened at the mere thought of such a blunder.

He turned to the old man. "If you've got any ideas, you might like to tell me, seeing as you're so keen for me to leave." Shrugging, the old man said, "Why don't you ask 'em which way?"

"Yeah, and you called *me* a dummy?" He turned away dismissively. "Although, it's probably something nearly as obvious," he said under his breath.

He crossed the floor to sit with his back against the wall, pondering the problem as he regarded the two arches and the strange-looking beings beside them.

The old man climbed out of his pile of straw and, with tin cup in hand, trotted over to the opposite corner to fill it from the tub. Returning to his nest he sat, cross-legged, nibbling morsels of stale bread and sipping from his cup, apparently deriving great enjoyment from the unfolding drama before him.

John looked across to him, pulled a cigarette from his packet and lit up. Taking a good draw, he blew the smoke towards the old man.

"Don't bother me none," said the old man, chuckling. "Ain't had this much fun since I poisoned the missus."

"You what!" John's face expressed a mixture of disgust and astonishment.

"Yup. Cyanide in her herbal tonic. Shut her up but good. Should'a seen her squirm, and the look on her stupid face. . ." He began to titter again.

John stood up suddenly, his visage darkening with anger. "Listen, you loathsome old buzzard. One more word, just one, and I swear I'm going to ..." With a finger upraised in warning, he was unable to come up with a suitable threat. "Well, you'll be sorry, that's all," he concluded lamely, and after continuing the stern look for a while longer, he slowly lowered himself back down against the wall, again to plumb the depths of the problem.

The old man was not in the slightest way daunted, producing a yellow- toothed grin which suggested he had elicited just the reaction he had hoped for.

John blew smoke into the air with an accentuated sigh and rested his head back against the wall, trying to rid himself of the frustration and rising anxiety which countered all attempts at clear and logical thought.

After a long period of silence, he turned his attention back to the stolid and strangely unobtrusive creatures who waited so dutifully. By this time he had decided that it was necessary to ask one question of each. That one was bound to lie, *there* lay the crux of this insidious conundrum; and the more he puzzled over it, the more elusive the solution became.

Crushing out his second cigarette and reaching for a third, he thought: Should I ask one of them if the other is the liar? No, of course not, that can't work ... Home - I want to go home. Yes, ask which way will take me home, and then ask the other ... what? If the answer the other gave me is true? Something along those lines. Maybe that's close. So, if the one on the left says this one, and the other creature says that's right ... No, then both would be lying. Oh God!

He looked up to find the old man watching him with keen interest. "Damn it," he objected. "Must you do that?"

"I suppose I could watch some television. But then I wouldn't want to disturb you, would I?"

"You've got a television?"

"Yeah, didn't I mention it? And a telephone to call up room service on, too. No, you idiot. Of course I don't have a television set. I must say, at this point I don't like your chances very much," he observed cheerfully.

John disliked intensely being a source of amusement for the old man, but even to think of this was a terrible distraction. He had to concentrate. He tried desperately to block all irrelevancies from his mind — to approach the problem again, calmly, logically.

One of them is the liar. Which one? Do I ask each of them if they're the liar? No, no, you idiot, of course not. Shit! Now I'm calling *myself* an idiot. It's the old man. If he disturbs me again, I'll kill him. What am I thinking of — of killing an old man? All I want is to go home — home! How bad could it be if I chose the wrong one? Not as bad as all that. I'd just have to play the game out, that's all. I can't think straight. It's a fifty–fifty chance. I could get lucky and then it would all be over. Christ!

In rising agitation he stood quickly and almost lost balance. The circulation in one leg had been cut off while he sat against the wall and was almost entirely numb, and as he hobbled in a tight circle, doing his best to restore life to the stricken limb, laughter rang around the stone walls.

"Why don't you give it up?" suggested the old man. "We both know you're bound to pick the wrong one. And, anyway, I think I could get used to having you around, now I've had a chance to get to know you. What do you say? You can have that corner over there," he said, pointing.

John slapped at his leg, feeling the uncomfortable sensation of circulation returning after too long being cut off. "Go to hell."

"Happy just where I am, thanks all the same. That mean you be leaving then?"

He made no reply, but turned once again to face the foreboding stone arches and was met with a startling surprise.

In each of them now were projected instantly recognisable images — images of home. In the left, the very game room where this nightmare had begun. In the right, the street corner where his local bank stood in full view, the street leading up the hillside and on to his home and family. It was more than he could bear.

In that moment he was sure that he glimpsed a solution to the puzzle. On an impulse born of longing, he called out to the stolid sentinel beside which the image of that familiar street led home. "How many fingers am I holding up?"

The reply came immediately, a sepulchral quality in the voice. "I don't know."

"What do you mean, you don't know?" he retorted urgently. "Are you blind?" He waved the two fingers emphatically above his head. The old man began cackling uncontrollably behind him, and too late, John clamped his hand over his mouth.

Again came the deep and dismal voice. "To the second, the meaning ought to be clear enough. I have said

I do not know. To the third, which I am not required to answer... Yes."

John's face turned ashen; a picture of shock, lost hope and dread. The old man's fit of laughter ceased unnaturally. "Now you've gone and done it," he remarked gravely.

No sooner had the old man spoken than a new caption appeared.

THIRTY SECONDS TO OPTION CLOSURE

He stared in horror as this was replaced by a digital clock display, counting implacably down towards zero.

"Choose, you fool," the old man called out from his corner, for the first time concern in his manner. "Hurry, before it's too late and you're trapped like me!"

John's eyes darted from one arch to the other, panic rising like a geyser beginning to boil, overwhelming the senses and threatening to override all reason.

"Fifteen seconds," chortled the old man. "I hope you're partial to gruel."

CLOSURE IMMINENT

John's focus settled on one arch in particular, where stood his local bank on the street corner, and somehow managing to break free of the paralysis which had gripped him, he lunged forward, a strangled cry of pure desperation escaping him as he raced to cover the intervening distance before his chance was gone.

At the moment of passing beneath the stone arch he vanished from sight; the raucous laughter which filled the room was abruptly silenced. The old man was captured as if in freeze–frame with his head thrown back in merriment and his hands held apart in mid-process of clapping, but his eyes now were dulled and bereft of animation.

For a time the scene remained that way, until, from a point high on the ceiling, a thin, dark line appeared to run, taking colour and substance in its wake, back and forth like the unravelling of a knitted garment, like pixels on a television screen expiring, one at a time, leaving only a growing number of empty spaces. The process gained momentum, the invasion of nothing growing at an increasing rate until just half of the room remained, and continued toward total erasure.

Landing at speed, John pitched headlong and fell heavily, skidding across the concrete at full–sprawl until he tipped clumsily from the edge of the curb, ending in a heap at the roadside. Somewhat stunned and smarting as a result of sundry bumps and grazes, he hauled himself dazedly to his feet, trying hard, beneath the glare of the corner street-light, to determine his whereabouts. . . Recognition struck like a hammer-blow.

He was just off the main street of Morgan Vale, the high stone walls of his bank right there, beside him. He turned and looked along the street which led up the hillside towards home, revelling in the familiarity of everything surrounding: The commonplace, everyday things which, not so long ago had merely been the backdrop in his dull and meaningless existence.

He let out a whoop of pure joy: It was all wonderful. A warm, secure, marvellous little haven. It was home town, and it was such an ineffable relief to be back. He whooped one more time, long and high and loud, and with a lump in his throat he set his feet back upon the footpath he had so many times trodden, and began the ascent toward family and home.

The night was cold and clear, perfectly still and sublimely stimulating, imbuing everything around with a mysterious aura so that it was like walking through a magic wonderland. Even the walking felt much more like floating on air. The word *euphoric* registered in his mind. He was well aware of his present state, and he rejoiced in the way it sharpened every faculty, every sense, bringing crystal clarity of perception, the body so in tune with itself and in perfect harmony with the world. Not since being a young man had he felt so invigorated, so thrilled in simply being alive.

He would not question the condition, preferring rather to simply enjoy the rare moment. In any case, it was eminently clear that the adversity he had endured had served to rekindle his zest for life. A heightened sense of well-being after coming through some kind of ordeal was not an uncommon occurrence. He was sure he had read it somewhere.

Some distance further along the way, while his mind was busily occupied with everything and nothing especially — merely relishing the strange–wonderful state of being, the full impact of what had taken place during the past several hours caught up with him, striking with a force which halted him mid-stride, and in that moment, again suspicion and unfathomable doubt took precedence. "Impossible," he whispered, standing stock still in bewilderment, looking along the street where houses stood in quiet darkness; every tree, power pole, fence and bush silhouetted or steeped in shadow. "So where have I been all this time? Have I at last lost my mind?"

The neighbourhood was unusually quiet, and not a single light burned in any house along the street. Even the usual drone of traffic along the main road was conspicuously absent. Never before had he experienced such an all-pervading silence as this. It seemed to press in quite unnaturally, the atmosphere heavy and sombre beneath an overcast sky, dense clouds obscuring the moon, barely visible but for a faint lambency.

It's late, he considered. I've never been out wandering the streets this late at night before. That's why it's so quiet. Everyone is asleep. "That must be it," he assured himself resuming the journey. But the extraordinary images of the day persisted; false memories, no doubt, but the fact that he could not account for the missing span of time was exceedingly disconcerting. He refused to believe that the affliction he had suffered all those years ago had returned. That was in the past; the doctors had viewed the possibility of a recurrence as unlikely. It was terribly vexing. The worst of it being that everything had become so tenuous. There were no certainties, nothing by which to fix perceived events in their place. Reality and non-reality were concepts which ordinary people should never need to grapple with, but now the two had no defining borders, so that thoughts, no matter how carefully they were arranged, remained only that, mere thoughts, without the certain foundation of proof.

It was — he struggled for understanding — as if he had been cast into a virtual world, where facts no longer existed.

Despite these formidable concerns, his feet unerringly continued to follow the path which, over the years, it had become second nature to do. But, still, except for the occasional streetlight, no other source of illumination was visible.

Street after street he negotiated, for the most part oblivious to his surroundings as his mind strove with difficulty to sort what was real from so much that was spurious and illogical, until, with some vaguely perceived irregularity, he stopped to survey the vicinity.

He looked carefully about, unsure of what it was he expected to find. The house he stood in front of was in its usual state of disrepair. Nothing odd about that. The thistle patch and– *that was it!* It was *gone.*

The rusting old VW Beetle its owner had tried for so long to sell— gone. Sold or perhaps carted away to the scrap-yard, finally. No matter, it seemed a good omen and something on which to take hold. A fix in time and space.

He lingered awhile longer before continuing on his way, permitting himself a few guarded thoughts of Margaret and the baby. The demands brought by the constant stress and confusion of the day had required that he steer clear of such poignant thoughts, or buckle under the strain. Even so, his thoughts had strayed on occasion, but with an end to the ordeal almost in sight, such strong yearnings would no longer be denied, and it seemed safe, now, so close to home, to give rein to some measure of anticipation.

He had to remind himself that, first, there would be the matter of his late return. Then the fact that he was without groceries or the money he had drawn from the bank, the last in their account. On that point all hell would break loose, he was sure.

As he neared the corner of his street, his pace dwindled. How would he explain? I'm sorry, dear, but I've been quite insane all afternoon. I lost all our money to a gambling machine that whisked me away to another dimension...

"I don't think so," he muttered, rounding the corner to begin the home stretch. "I'm for it."

For it or not, in so close proximity to home his pace quickened again as, irresistibly, he was drawn forward by the mounting visceral tension accompanying every step closer he came.

The house was within sight now, and nothing stood in his way. After the terrible experience he had just been through, he knew he would find the strength and determination to see them safely through their present adversities. He remembered his idea of finding work out of town, whether it was at some suburban factory or way out bush, and he knew that he could do it. Whatever the price, he would see his family right. Things would turn out just fine.

Approaching the house he saw that, like all the rest, it lay in darkness. Both sound asleep, he guessed. He would have to wake Margaret and apologise, tell her that everything was all right and that he was sorry for causing her to worry. An explanation would be difficult, but he would cross that bridge when he came to it. Maybe the news of his decision to find work would circumvent the need — or not. He was home and nothing else mattered quite as much.

He slid his key into the lock and turned it, switching on the light as he entered. The lounge room was tidy and spotlessly clean, as he might have expected - it had been Margaret's intention to clean the house while he was out. He closed the front door and crossed to the kitchen, flicking on the light switch as he entered.

He was hungry, but that could wait. As a temporary measure he poured himself a glass of milk and drank it straight down. Now came the difficult part, and when he had rinsed the glass clean under the tap and stood it beside the sink, he turned and strode determinedly towards the main bedroom at the end of the passageway.

At the bedroom door he paused to take a fortifying breath, then, as quietly as he could, he turned the handle and pushed open the door. "Honey?" he called softly. "Honey, I'm home. I need to talk to you. Can I turn the light on?" He waited. "Dear? Are you awake?" When no reply came he switched on the light, discovering an empty, neatly made bed. The unexpected scene left him standing, mouth agape in total surprise.

He backed up two paces, opened the door of the nursery and switched on the light. Neither mother nor baby were there.

Guilt-stricken, he hurried to the telephone where it hung on the kitchen wall. If something had happened while he was gone he would never be able to forgive himself. He reached to lift the receiver, only then remembering that they had been disconnected over a month ago.

"Sweet Jesus. What could have happened?" he said, close to panic. He looked up to the clock above the refrigerator. It was two-thirty in the morning. Too late to go knocking on neighbours' doors, but was there any option?

He strode out across the lawn and onto the street, leaving the front door wide open and the house singularly ablaze with light. He looked to the Wilson's house across the street. The absence of a car in the driveway indicated that no one was at home.

He walked over to the Jeffrey's, next door along, and found the same situation. Not one car did he observe in the whole street. To the Overmyre's, then, their neighbours to the right. They didn't own a car, so this time he would at least try and raise someone. He stepped up to the door and without hesitation knocked loudly, the sound carrying in the stillness of the night, resounding up and down the empty street. He knocked again. "Hello. I'm sorry to disturb you. It's John Edwards from next door."

There was no response.

"My wife and child," he called again. "Did you see them leave the house? . . . Hello!"

In desperation he turned and walked back out to the street, shouting, "Is anybody listening? My wife and child are gone. Can somebody help me? Please, does anybody know what happened?" He was met with absolute silence. In the dead of night he strained to listen for the slightest sound, only to hear his own heartbeat. "Anybody! Anybody at all!" he cried in anguish, hoping that at least someone might call the police. "Help me!"

When the echoes of his plaintive call had died away he was left standing in the middle of the street, arms limp by his sides, looking helplessly around at the deserted neighbourhood. . . and something deep inside told him that he was completely alone.

He stood that way for some minutes, until his weary legs began to ache and he was forced to walk over to the curb and sit at the front of his house. For the moment his mind refused even to consider the possibilities of the situation. There could be no questioning his own sanity. It had gone way too far beyond that point already. There was only what he was experiencing now, and if or how he should respond to it. At best it might be a terrible dream.

He cut short a reproachful chuckle and reached into his pocket for his cigarettes and lighter, lit one up and expelled smoke into the chilly night air. He toyed with the lighter in his hand, absently, as he stared out over the roof-tops into the starless sky, despair and desolation steering his thoughts through unending convolutions where grief and confusion began slowly to tighten like a ravelling knot.

From the brink of the abyss, he drew back with a jolt. *The lighter!* He held it up to catch the light spilling from the house, its nacreous finish capturing the light and transmuting it into a soft radiance of shifting colours - the emblazoned Omnicorp logo prominent in gold.

Buoyed, his flagging energies rallied around the physical existence of this one object, proof that, somehow, what he had experienced was no delusion - no mere phantom generated by the workings of an unbalanced mind. It was *real*.

Or was it? Again lurked that enervating doubt.

He could have picked it up at any stage of what may well have been a psychotic episode, his deranged thought processes deftly weaving it into the fabric of the delusion. No, a cigarette-lighter proved nothing.

He sat at the roadside, alone and miserable beyond any misery he remembered. How much have I lost, he thought to himself. What is there left for me to live for?

Some distance off, he spied movement. Something in the deep shadows at the base of a timber paling fence. A cat, he supposed, but, no, it was too large for a cat. A dog then. The only living thing he had seen since his return.

He followed its stealthy progress until it emerged from the shadows opposite. Black and sleek-looking, it was as large as a Labrador but resembled nothing he had ever seen before, except ... yes, those strange, unearthly figurines carved in miniature atop the machine.

His blood ran cold as it halted and turned to regard him with piercing, emerald green eyes. It was vaguely humanoid, crouched on all fours though, and its face, small and devilish, expressed a kind of malevolence as if a dull mind was all that prevented it from achieving truly evil status. It studied him for a time, casually, forestalling John rising to retreat inside the house.

A sound some distance away to John's left, drew its attention. It hunkered down against the ground and peered intently along the street where movement was detected. Then with an air of menace it snapped its powerful jaws closed, the sound of gnashing teeth leaving no doubt as to its capability before it disappeared back into the night, away from the streetlights.

At the crest of the hill, beneath the glare of a corner streetlight, a group of three, large apelike creatures loped along together. With great relief he watched as they turned down another street and began to move away down the slope.

Turning back again he saw that the small beast had gone, but now his body quaked with the coursing of cold dread through his veins, sapping all volition to the last. He sat in fear, unable to flee, gripped by a spreading paralysis which threatened to numb his entire being. And then, as if from far away, a voice echoed through the myriad, vacant corridors of his mind. It was his wife's voice, iterating the strident warning she had given as he left home that afternoon: "You dare go near those machines ... You dare go near those machines ... You dare go near those machines ... "

High above, the obscuring clouds suddenly separated to reveal a moon full–round and bright — much brighter, much larger than it should have been — and over the face of it there appeared a holographic image, a tri-star arrangement within a golden circle. At its centre, a double helix, rotating slowly.

As he watched, the clouds continued to disperse, growing ever more tenuous until all trace of them had disappeared. What remained was blackness - the Omnicorp branded moon and an endless, black void which overwhelmed the senses and, with icy fingers, tugged darkly at the soul.

Then appeared the caption which he knew had to come:

GAME CONTINUES

INSERT ONE MONETARY UNIT AND TRY AGAIN

end

AN AFTERTHOUGHT
BY THE AUTHOR

and

The Solution to the Riddle of the Portals

THE WRITING OF *For Your Pleasure* was for me a chance to emulate some of the greatly imaginative writers I used to enjoy as a young man. It was also an opportunity for me to express my concerns about the nature of pokie machines and their dubious function in society. It was not, however, until I decided to try and get a couple of snapshots of machines for the cover of this book, that my vague cynicism turned to outright suspicion.

My first surprise came at a local hotel, when, at the sight of my little pocket camera, I was set upon as though I was some type of criminal engaged in espionage... and the little drama was re- enacted in each of the next three pokie venues I visited. In fairness, the individual *privacy act* was quoted to me, *one time*, but when I suggested I snap only the machines, perhaps at a more suitable time, some other excuse was always conjured up.

....It soon became evident that it was the pokie machine companies who were setting the rules, so it was they whom I approached next.

I was learning to be less naive by this time, and over the telephone I simply requested brochures of some of their more fancy-looking machines. Of course, when asked to identify myself, I had to tell them I was a writer looking for a cover design, and that's when their voices - their entire attitudes, in fact - turned ice cold.

The much repeated response became: "Who are you from?" No doubt suspecting I was a journalist, sniffing out information for some negatively slanted story... which I considered to be a conclusion leapt at a tad hastily. There certainly is a lot of paranoia in the business! More than that, secrecy and even deception.

By now I was becoming suspicious. Cynicism gave way to something closer akin to disgust, which never would have occurred if this strange behaviour hadn't been so evident wherever I asked a simple question. So, what's going on? Aren't these machines the innocent amusement providers we were encouraged to believe? We know the Government is in it for the dough. At least they don't pretend anything different, do they? Great little revenue-raisers, the pokies... though I'd love to see some benefits: improved hospital services, for example. But *there's* a whole other subject!

Needless to say (because of the appearance of the front cover) I never did get the photographs I needed. I got tired of being ejected from pubs and clubs, and I sensed that I might soon be facing legal intimidation, which, although I would have enjoyed a fight, I simply couldn't afford in terms of time and energy. But why didn't I simply walk in with a camera and sneak a few shots, you're asking? Well that would be wrong... wouldn't it? I was certainly made to feel as though it was.

The naivety and presumption of we citizens, to suppose that it would be okay to take a couple of snapshots inside our local pub. Can't allow people to walk around acting of their own volition, can we? Tantamount to anarchy, that!

And it's the regular occurrence of situations such as that, which ever reminds me of at least one of the reasons why I took up writing in the first place.

But now to something more fun. For those of you who, like me, can't let your mind rest until a puzzle is solved, the solution to John's dilemma is described on the following page And no fair peeking if you haven' yet read the story.

THE SOLUTION TO THE RIDDLE OF THE PORTALS.

I FIRST CAME ACROSS this elegant little problem during my high school days. (Christies Beach High School, if you're wondering. South Australia.) Who showed it to me I have since forgotten, but it is such a lovely piece of logic and I'm so pleased to have found the perfect scenario in which to present it to you. In fact, the protagonist had already stumbled into the particular situation before I was aware of what riddle the machine would set for him.

The tactic employed for revealing the correct choice is almost obvious, infuriatingly so because it can be simultaneously elusive; and I would hate to be in a situation such as John's, having a cell- mate continually distracting, a clock counting down the seconds to when his escape route would be snatched away, and the added jeopardy of making the wrong choice, thereby being confronted with yet another nasty surprise. But he was on the right track.

He recognised that he first needed to distinguish which sentinel was the liar and which told the truth. The trick, with only two questions allowed, is in the economy of questions and the highest yield of pertinent information from them. So, naming the sentinels A and B...

Ask A how B will answer the question: "Which portal will take me home?"

*If A says LEFT and B answers the question with LEFT, then A told the truth. Therefore, B lied and the RIGHT portal is the correct one to take him home.

*If A says RIGHT and B replies LEFT, then A is the liar, B told the truth and LEFT is correct. The rule applies for the remainder of the permutations.

cheers and adieu!